WRECKED!

"We're going to crash!" screamed Dale. "Look out!"

Flash tore at the wheel frantically. The jetcar did not respond.

He could hear the cacophony of tortured metal, then the smash of plyoglass, the burning of plyolact left on the copolypetrol surface, and the wrenching screech of impact as they hit.

The giant forest plants above them wavered. The plyoglass windscreen seemed to melt like ice sheets in a nuclear blast. The zarcar turned over on the forest growth and came to a shuddering, jolting halt.

"Flash!" screamed Dale.

Then there was absolute silence.

FLASH GORDON

Alex
Raymond's
Original Story

THE TIME TRAP
OF MING XIII

Adapted by Con Steffanson

Co-published by Avon Books
and King Features Syndicate

AVON
PUBLISHERS OF BARD, CAMELOT, DISCUS, EQUINOX AND FLARE BOOKS

The TIME TRAP OF MING XIII is an original publication of
Avon Books. This work has never before appeared in book
form.

AVON BOOKS
A division of
The Hearst Corporation
959 Eighth Avenue
New York, New York 10019

Copyright © 1974 by King Features Syndicate, Inc.
Co-published by Avon Books and King Features Syndicate, Inc.

ISBN: 0-380-00111-X

First Avon Printing, September, 1974.

AVON TRADEMARK REG. U.S. PAT. OFF. AND
FOREIGN COUNTRIES, REGISTERED TRADEMARK—
MARCA REGISTRADA, HECHO EN CHICAGO, U.S.A.

Printed in the U.S.A.

THE TIME TRAP
OF MING XIII

CHAPTER 1

They were deep in the primeval forest, not far from Arboria on the superway from the spaceport, when the trouble began. The power in the jetcar failed. Then, abruptly, it returned.

"What's the matter, Flash?" asked Dale Arden, turning to the driver. She was a slender, dark-haired girl in her early twenties dressed in a pale-green stretch blouse, wide crimson belt, and informal spacetravel skirt.

Flash Gordon turned to her with a frown. "I don't know, Dale," he said. "I thought for a moment I was losing jet thrust." He was a strappingly muscular man with curly blond hair, blue eyes, and a deep solar tan. He wore a one-piece military uniform with the World Council ranking of colonel on the collar.

Dale frowned. "This is a mighty lonely part of the forest." Strange tropical vegetation towered above the curved superway as it wound through the Forest Kingdom of Mongo. Giant specimens of Earth's ferns and conifers abounded in the region.

"I guess the thrust pack is all right," Flash said, testing the foot pedal. "I'm not used to this hydrogen-powered model of Zarkov's."

Dale was lost in deep thought. She stared out at the oranges and lavenders and beiges that seemed to glow among the lush vegetation.

"Cat got your tongue?" asked Flash.

"When I've been away, I always forget how beautiful the trees of the forest kingdom really are," she said, sighing.

"Erratic evolutionary development," Flash said. "Earth plant growth followed a more leisurely pattern of change.

7

Mongo's suffered a slowdown, due to the planet's erratic cooling process, and then a quick speedup."

"Oh, I know all that," said Dale. She fell silent.

"That isn't what you're really thinking about, is it?"

"No." Dale smiled. "I'm thinking how glad I'll be to see our old friends on Mongo. Prince Barin. Dr. Zarkov."

"It'll be like old home week." Flash chuckled. "Doc Zarkov sounded just the same when we talked to him by laserphone from the Spaceport Inn, maybe a little louder and boomier than ever, but that's Zarkov's style."

"I don't know how you talk to him," Dale said. "It's always hydrogen packs or suspension systems or thrust pedals. I can never make head nor tail out of what he's saying. Sometimes I'd just like to pull his beard and make him scream."

Flash laughed good-naturedly.

As they shot along the newly constructed, delicately cambered roadway, only the swishing sound of the plyolact tires whispering over the surface of the slick copolypetrol pavement broke the silence of the giant forest about them. Now and then a gold-and-red bird flashed into view, only to vanish instantly amidst the purple and beige of the trees and vines. They were alardactyls, mostly, similar to Earth's flying mammals—strange beasts with brilliant silver eyes that turned gold when they sighted prey.

"Something's bothering you," Flash said suddenly.

Dale glanced at him. "Yes. I am worried."

He laughed. "That's obvious. But I don't know why you should be."

Dale was silent a moment. Then she said: "There have been so many delays."

"Delays?" Flash kept his eye on the road. The superway wound lazily through towering ferns and gigantic conifers on either side. He could feel that slight lack of thrust in the pedal under his foot. And then, almost immediately, the power was back. "What delays?"

"Oh, the delay in getting the jetcar papers, for example."

"That's just bureaucratic paper juggling, Dale. Nothing to worry about."

"And before that. The long flight from Earth's system."

8

"Sun spots, Dale. *Our* solar sun spots. You can't blame that on Mongo."

"I suppose not." Dale frowned.

"Well?"

"And then there was that unexpected traffic tieup in the spaceport."

"Population density, Dale." Flash laughed. "Even on Mongo."

"You haven't said a word about that break-in at the Spaceport Inn."

Flash frowned. He glanced at Dale. "A simple burglary, Dale. They have cat burglars on Mongo as well as on Earth."

"I don't like it at all—and to have the two of them so—well—so strange."

"Strange? Oh, you mean the innkeeper's daughter and her description of them? Weird dress? They were actors, just as they said they were, doing a science-fiction play."

"I don't know," Dale said musingly.

"You know what?" Flash asked with a grin.

"What?"

"You're just being a worry wart."

Dale frowned and slid down into the plyoform seat, folding her arms irritably over her chest.

"What would be the purpose of delaying our visit to Arboria and Prince Barin?" Flash asked after a moment.

"I don't know," snapped Dale. "Forget I said it."

Flash was watching the dials on the jetcar's console. Thrust: okay. Hydrogen content: half. Reactor well: okay. Heat exchange: pressure good. E.T.A.: minus fifty-five seconds.

He drew up sharply. "Something's wrong, Dale! We're losing speed!"

Dale glanced at the Estimated Time of Arrival readout in the digital port. "Almost a minute slow! What's happened?"

The digital port spun with figures: 150s 200s.

Flash pushed on the thrust pedal The figures continued to speed by in the digital port. 250s. 300s.

"We're losing power!"

The jetcar suddenly shuddered and wobbled on the su-

9

perway as if the road itself were trying to buck it off. Flash gripped the wheel desperately. The jetcar steadied down to a straight course.

"What was that all about?" Dale's face was white.

"I don't know," Flash admitted.

"Is the roadbed pitted?" She peered ahead through the plyoglass windscreen. The superway stretched out ahead of them like a band of ribbon laid through the wild growth of vegetation. There were no pockmarks in the slick, expertly fabricated copoly-petrol surface.

"Impossible," said Flash. "Mongo's minerals make a firm bond with the carbon molecule. Copoly-petrol simply cannot break up like Earth's macadam base."

"Then the trouble must be in the car," Dale whispered, glancing about her at the expertly engineered interior of the revolutionary hydrogen-powered zarcar—named after Dr. Zarkov and his scientists who had designed it.

"Absolutely negative," snapped Flash. "This is the finest piece of equipment made on Mongo. According to Doc Zarkov, anyway. Hydrogen reactor made of lexmat, the most durable metal in the whole Mongo system. Jet thrusters of litelep, the least weighty alloy known. Indestructible tires of plyolact, combining the elasticity of Mongo's famous milktree sap and the durability of plyomatt. Zarkov designed it. There's nothing that could go wrong!"

Dale shook her head helplessly. "I know, Flash." Her eyes widened. "Hey! What's that odor?"

Flash sniffed. The zarcar was suddenly filled with a smell that was utterly foreign to his nostrils.

"It's unlike anything I ever smelled before," he said, sniffing hesitantly. "Oranges? Loquats? The tang of tomato vines in the rain? Dale, it's all three smells combined. I don't know what it is!"

The forest on either side of them hurtled by, the superway trembling beneath the weight of the speeding jetcar. As abruptly as the smell had come, it vanished, and they were once again breathing Mongo's slightly saline air, with its additional units of nitrogen.

Dale opened her mouth to cry out, but gripped Flash's arm instead. "My ears!"

Flash held onto the wheel of the jetcar. "Mine, too!" he cried. "It's not a sound, it's an agonizing pain! What is it?"

10

"I can't stand the vibrations."

"Overtones! Beyond the audibility range of the human ear," gasped Flash, straining to keep from screaming. "It's some extremely high vibration, a fantastically powerful resonance, some tremendous shaking."

"My head!" Dale slumped into the plyoform cushion. Her eyes closed.

Then, as quickly as it had come, the pain left Flash's ears.

Dale opened her eyes and sat up.

"It's all over," Flash muttered. "What do you think it was?"

"First a weird smell, and then that sound you can't even hear." Dale trembled. "I don't think we should have come here today, Flash."

"Nonsense!" said Flash. "It's just your imagination."

Dale never had a chance to respond.

The jetcar swerved and tore away from Flash's iron control. He twisted the steering wheel over and over to the left, but the zarcar continued of its own accord to the right, careening off the ribbon of superway, slashing through the blue forest into the lavender-and-orange mists.

"We're going to crash!" screamed Dale. "Look out!"

Flash tore at the wheel frantically. The jetcar did not respond.

He could hear the cacophony of tortured metal, then the smash of plyoglass, the burning of plyolact left on the copoly-petrol surface, and the wrenching screech of impact as they hit.

The giant forest plants above them wavered. The plyoglass windscreen seemed to melt like ice sheets in a nuclear blast. The zarcar turned over on the forest growth and came to a shuddering, jolting halt.

"Flash!" screamed Dale.

Then there was absolute silence.

CHAPTER 2

In the measureless dimension of the primeval forest there was almost complete quiescence. Flash opened his eyes and found himself staring into Mongo's yellowish clay-colored sky. The branches of the giant plants waved in a sudden movement of air over the surface of the planet.

Instantly he recalled the crash of the jetcar and Dale's cry. Shaking his head to rid it of the brief pain he had suffered, he sat up. Dale was slumped against the plyoform-cushioned interior. Her eyes were closed. Flash could not see any wounds on her skin.

"Dale," he called anxiously.

His voice seemed to hang in the air. The sound reverberated and echoed for a moment, repeating itself again and again. Then it faded away.

Flash raised his head and looked around.

The plyoglass conetop of the zarcar had been thrown aside by the shock of its impact with an enormous fern stalk a good eight feet across. The jetcar's chassis was lying on its side, wedged between two upthrusts of a shalelike rock that was probably drogue ore, the type of mineral Mongo's scientific fraternity used to formulate drogiron, a kind of annealed steel.

"Dale!"

She stirred and opened her eyes. "Flash!"

"Are you all right?" Flash asked anxiously, shaking her by the arm.

"Yes." She blinked. "I seem to be alive. That's the main thing." She glanced around. "What happened?"

"I lost control," said Flash ruefully. "The jetcar just went off the superway."

12

Dale raised her head and tried to look out through the windscreen. "It's so quiet out there," she murmured.

"I'm going to get out of the car and see if I can find out what went wrong. Are you all right now?"

"Yes, yes," said Dale impatiently. "Don't worry about me."

Flash reached toward the doorhandle and tugged at it. The jetcar had landed half on its side and half on its frame. It lay at a forty-five-degree angle. The sudden redistribution of Flash's weight when he moved caused the hulk to creak and groan and settle to the left. The frame crashed down onto the forest surface with a heavy thump and a sigh. Dust motes boiled up.

Flash unbuttoned the doorpack and pulled out a handkerchief. He held it over his nose for protection.

"Dusty," he said.

Flash opened the driver's door and climbed out of the jetcar, glancing up and down the length of the forest as he did so. Birds, beasts—every live thing had been frightened away by the noise of the crash. In the distance an alardactyl wheeled in a silvery arc, catching the glint of Mongo's mustard sun at zenith, and plunged into the lavender foliage.

Dale sat up and began patting her hair back into place. She called out, "I'll try to use the laserphone to contact Arboria."

"Right," said Flash.

He slammed the driver's door shut and stood by the side of the zarcar, looking down at the wheels in amazement. Or rather he found himself looking down at the portion of the jetcar where the wheels were supposed to be.

There were none there!

Flash straightened and glanced about him in dismay. The wheels had apparently been torn off by the crash. He frowned and walked around the jetcar to view the other side. There he stood in perplexity.

"What is it, Flash?" Dale asked. She was looking out through her window at him in surprise.

"The wheels were torn off—actually torn off!"

"Torn off?" Dale repeated. "That doesn't make sense."

"It certainly doesn't." The dust that boiled up around

13

the car had settled now. Flash went down on his knees to examine a small pile of it that lay near the off-rear-wheel vent.

He picked up a handful of the very fine dust and held it in his palm. With his left forefinger and thumb he pinched a bit of it and rubbed it between his fingertips. He could feel its strange consistency—not sand, not dirt. Nor was it actually dust.

It was pulverized—finely pulverized—metal of some kind!

"Dale!" Flash cried. "The dust we saw. It isn't dust at all. It's some kind of metallic powder."

"Metallic powder?"

Flash got down on his stomach and peered in at the bottom of the jetcar's frame. And instantly he knew what had happened.

"I can't believe it! The whole suspension system of the car—the shocks, the axles, the springs, everything under the car—is gone!"

Dale leaned out the window and stared at the ground where the pile of dust lay. "Maybe that's what the dust is."

Flash rose, his eyes narrowed. "That's what I'm thinking too. Sure. Powdered metal. The entire suspension system has been turned to dust!" He stood there, looking back down the superway from where they had come. He could see one of the wheels made of zarplast—a special plastic Zarkov had formulated out of Mongo's minerals—lying in the middle of the roadway with its plyolact tire intact. "But look! The tire is perfectly all right."

Dale climbed out. The jetcar rocked slightly as she jumped to the ground and came over to stand by Flash.

"Maybe that was what we smelled—the metal turning to dust. And that high-pitched inaudible sound may have been what caused it to disintegrate."

Flash nodded. "It's a logical assumption. Did you get anyone on the laserphone?"

"It's gone dead."

"The laser rod is mounted to the frame of the jetcar," said Flash musingly. "I suppose the rod was pulverized, too."

14

Dale lifted her head. "Sh!" She was poised alertly, frowning. "Did you hear that?"

"I heard nothing," said Flash, staring at the mound of dust in his hand. "Look. If this is metal fatigue, it is the tiredest metal I've ever seen. Frankly, I'm stumped. The entire suspension system, everything made out of metal, has simply disintegrated into dust. What happened to it? Is there some poisonous effluvia in the air? Did that resonating sound we heard affect the metal? What turned it to dust? A laser ray? An antimatter beam?"

"Well, we'll have to ask Dr. Zarkov when we see him," Dale said brightly. "I'm sure he'd love to tell us."

Flash brooded at the wrecked car. "Maybe his design had a few flaws in it."

"This isn't getting us any nearer to Arboria. If we're going to have to walk, we'd better start. It's a long way."

Flash rubbed his chin thoughtfully. "We didn't meet anyone on the superway, did we? I mean there's not much hope of getting a lift, is there?"

Dale shook her head.

"Then let's get going."

"Flash! Look out!" screamed Dale.

Flash pivoted quickly. He saw nothing, but suddenly he sensed a high-pitched resonance in the air similar to the vibrations he and Dale had felt when the jetcar had bucked. Instinctively he clapped his hands to his ears. His head felt as if it were being pressed between two boulders.

"Take cover!" he cried to Dale. "We're—we're—" His eye caught a flash of light off in the forest nearby. He could not distinguish exactly what caused it, but the resonance seemed to emanate from that point.

"We're under attack, Dale! Get behind the jetcar—hurry!"

The air suddenly blossomed into liquid flame and the magnetic force of a beam projected toward Flash knocked him backward into a giant fern stalk. He crawled around and crouched behind it to get out of the direct line of the ray.

And then, suddenly, everything was very quiet once again.

CHAPTER 3

Cautiously, Flash emerged from behind the fern. Dale still hid behind the jetcar, where it lay canted slightly on a tangle of forest roots and dead branches.

The air about them was very calm now, as if it had never been touched by the heat and power of the strange ray.

"Dale," he called to her, "are you all right?"

"Yes," she answered, raising her head. "Is it safe to come out?"

"Strange," Flash mused, without answering her. "That ray simply stunned me for a moment."

"I'm not hurt, either." Dale walked around the rear of the jetcar and joined Flash in the clearing.

"Probably the same ray disintegrated the metal in the jetcar's suspension system. But if it did that, why didn't it hurt us?"

Dale shook her head, glancing around at the forest with puzzled apprehension.

Flash pointed his gloved hand toward a heavy curtain of foliage. "It came from that direction, wouldn't you say?" The dense cluster of vegetation lay not far from the superway as it curved and dipped through a formation of light-purple klang outcropping. Klang resembled Earth's granite rock, except that it was purple with brown specks.

"I saw a flash of light," said Dale, "and then the air seemed to resonate."

Flash began walking toward the dense undergrowth. "Let's go see if we can find the machine that projected the ray. I assume, at least, that it was a ray of some kind."

Dale stopped dead in her tracks. "Look!"

"Two men," muttered Flash. His hand immediately sought the blaster pistol in the leather holster at his belt.

The two men stood some distance from them, but it was easy to see them, even in the thick wooded growth of the forest surrounding them. One was tall and slim, the other short and fat.

They wore paramilitary uniforms. Flash distinguished sleeves that fastened in tightly at the wrists, military trousers that bagged at the knees and ankles, and then disappeared into shiny boots. The uniforms were chartreuse, but the texture of the material was not identifiable at a distance.

What appeared to be ammo belts with pouches spaced at intervals were fastened around their waists. Their heads were bare. Flash did not recognize the uniform and knew that it came from no known combat unit in the galaxy and allied systems.

Although the men's faces were not close enough to distinguish clearly, Flash got the impression that they both had mustaches. Their flesh seemed to resemble the chartreuse attire, being of a kind of yellowish tone.

"They did it," said Dale positively.

"Don't worry, I'll get them!" Flash said, starting through the undergrowth. "They can't get away with this!"

"They're armed!" cried Dale. "Don't let them hurt you."

"I won't," Flash promised. He pushed aside branches and vines. A hollow ravine separated him from the cleared flatland upon which the two strangers stood. Flash plunged down a slope and made his way through crimson-and-gold bushes.

He came up the other side of the draw and saw the two men more clearly now. They were standing exactly where they had been a moment before. Behind him, Flash saw Dale standing on the other side of the ravine, looking at the two uniformed men.

"Hey!" called Flash. "Are you the two men who wrecked our car?"

There was no response.

"Well?" Flash called out, making his way toward them through the thick undergrowth.

The two men conferred briefly. Then, with the quickness of a magician's illusion, they vanished into thin air!

Flash halted, staring. He passed his gloved hand over his eyes and blinked rapidly. Then he stared into the forest

17

and saw that the two men had indeed disappeared from sight.

Stunned, Flash turned to Dale. "Did you see that?"

Dale's face was perplexed. "I saw it. I was looking at the two of them and they simply went up in a puff."

"An optical illusion?" Flash pondered. "I want to check."

Dale ran through the undergrowth after him. "I'm coming with you."

Flash waited for her to join him and then the two of them proceeded through the tangled brush until they came to the spot where the two men had stood.

It was a small clearing in the middle of thick and twisted combinations of ferns, vines, scrub brush, and tall slender umbrella-topped minitrees that thrust briefly into the air. The lavenders, oranges, and crimson colors dazzled the eye.

"They could have run into the cover of the trees," Dale said thoughtfully.

"No way." Flash shook his head. "I was looking right at them. They simply vanished."

"I saw them go, too." Dale sighed. "It was just an idea."

"Perhaps they weren't really here," Flash said. "I mean—mirrors? Video projection? A holograph?"

Dale walked about the clearing, her eyes on the ground. "Here," she exclaimed.

Flash watched her as she knelt down and touched a small tuft of mongospike, a type of forest grass that grew only on the planet of Mongo.

"What are you talking about?"

"Broken," she said, pointing to the sheathed and jointed sections of the spiked purple grass. "Somebody was standing here very recently."

Flash picked up the tuft of mongospike and studied it. Then he searched the area with his eyes until he came to a stretch of Mongo's puce-colored soil. There was a footprint there, made by the shape of a military boot.

"There was a man here—one of the men I saw. And here's another print. They both wore boots."

Dale nodded.

Flash searched the humus more thoroughly, examining

the tufts of mongospike. "The prints are isolated right here," he said. "There are no tracks leading away from the spot where we saw them."

He stood up, stretching his muscles.

"Well, what do we do now?" Dale asked. "If they mean us no harm. . . ." She let her voice drop.

Flash looked into her eyes. "How can we be sure of that? Just because that ray they projected at us was a stunner and not a destroyer, how can we be sure the next one won't burn us the way the first one burned the metal of the zarcar?"

Dale shook her head in dismay. "We can't be sure, Flash."

The sight of the superway in the forest caught Flash's eye in the distance. He watched the point a moment longer, then grabbed Dale's arm.

"You see?" He pointed at the curtain of foliage.

"What?"

"From here it's a straight line to the jetcar. See the hood? All right. Let your eye travel beyond that point. Straight ahead, in a direct line. What do you see?"

Dale let her eye move along the same plane. "Why, it's a curve in the superway, Flash."

"Exactly. Right where we began to have trouble with the zarcar."

Dale turned to stare at him.

"That means they stood here, aiming the ray at us through the trees! They watched us crash. And then they stunned us. Why didn't they kill us?"

"I don't mind admitting it, Flash," said Dale in a tremulous voice. "I'm scared!"

CHAPTER 4

The two men in the iridescent chartreuse uniforms stood for a moment under an enormous fern tree, catching their breaths. They had been running through the forest. The purples and reds shimmered in the light of Mongo's seventh sun.

"Kial," said the fat one, gasping. "Why did we have to run through the forest in such a huge circle?"

The tall slender one stared at his companion as if he were a fool. "Dummy," he said. "To throw Flash Gordon off the trail!"

"But he couldn't see us when we pushed the button on our time belts."

"No," said Kial impatiently.

The fat one smiled. "Anyway, he didn't catch us."

Kial chuckled craftily. "And he won't stumble onto the Tempendulum, either. Right, Lari?"

Lari blinked in surprise. "I see. You thought maybe he would follow us to the Tempendulum."

"Your marvelous intellect constantly amazes me, Lari! Simply amazes me."

Lari smiled. His curling mustaches twitched and big dimples spread over his sallow complextion. "But, Kial, if he couldn't see us, how could he follow us?"

"Dummy! If he'd tried to follow us, he'd have gone right past where we were and he'd have stumbled onto the Tempendulum."

"Yeah," said Lari, light dawning.

"Now, come on," snapped Kial. "We've got to get back and report in!"

Lari's face fell. Two tears squeezed out of his little black eyes. "I'm afraid, Kial."

"What's to be afraid of?"

"The emperor," cried Lari. "When he finds out we haven't delayed Flash Gordon for good—"

"Let me handle this," said Kial, throwing out his chest and starting to walk through the forest. "The emperor is a hard man, but a just man."

Lari trotted through the undergrowth after Kial, having a hard time keeping up. "Yeah."

"Yeah, what?" Kial repeated with annoyance.

"Yeah. A just man."

Kial growled in his throat. "That's what we've been taught to say, anyway." He let a sly smile cross his face, tilting his mustaches up.

"He's going to disintegrate us when he finds out we've let Flash Gordon get away!" sobbed Lari.

Kial frowned and slowed to a walk. "It would be nice if we could stay here, wouldn't it?" he asked, looking around at the giant plants of the forest.

In silence, the two of them continued onward, more and more slowly.

Finally, they stopped and gazed through a gap in the undergrowth.

"There it is," said Lari sadly.

"Right where we left it," Kial agreed.

Hidden in the thick and high-topped trees was a hemispherical structure the size of an ordinary two-story building. It was built of metal alloy, surfaced with a bright sheen that caught the stray rays of Mongo's seventh sun filtering down through the leaves and sent them flashing into the trees in rainbow-hued arcs.

Sharp metallic vanes partitioned the hemispheroid, running from the zenith all the way down to the equator, where the structure joined the earth. There were twelve vanes, all joining at the top of the sphere. A cone extended straight from the joint into the sky.

Entry into the hemispheroid was afforded by a porthole that could be seen at the bottom of the metallic covering.

"If only we could use it now to get back to the future," Lari mused, staring at the metal demiglobe.

"That's traitorous talk!" snapped Kial. "We must stay in this historical era until we make sure Flash Gordon does not get to Arboria."

21

Lari's eyes narrowed. "A minute ago you spoke as if you'd like to stay here forever."

Kial scoffed harshly. "Don't remind me of that, Lari."

"All right." Lari sighed. "Let's get into the Tempendulum and report to the emperor." He wiped the perspiration off his face.

Kial walked through the mongospike to the metallic hemispheroid and climbed through the porthole, with Lari following. Inside the hollow dome, a subdued purplish light glowed from a large instrument console set up at one end of the circular room.

Hanging from the ceiling at the top of the dome was a large pendulumlike metal rod extending down almost to floor level, ending in a heart-shaped metal weight. The pendulum was still.

Floating in the air somewhere between their heads and the top of the dome was a large, oval miniglobe of impenetrable shiny black, inside of which could be heard a slight hissing. A glow seemed to emanate from the globe, as if it contained millions of volts of electromagnetic energy, or the power of thousands of light rays of heat.

Kial moved quickly to the console and studied the dials and digital readout ports. A purple glow shimmered behind the dials and numbers in the ports. Mounted at one side of the console was a large vidscreen, which was dark now. Dials and a complex system of computer connections fed into it.

Near the pendulum were two astro-seats tilted at rest position. Shiny straps dangled from the arms of the seats.

Lari strolled over and sank into one of them, closing his eyes as he wiggled his toes inside his boots.

"Okay," Kial said importantly. "I've got the perichron laservid connected. I want you—" he turned and saw Lari lazing in the astro-seat—"Dummy Get up here. We've got work to do."

Lari jumped to his feet. "Sure, Kial! Anything you say." The astro-seat rocked slowly as he hurried across the surface of the dome's metallic flooring.

"Come on!" Kial's face was flushed. "I want you to make our report to the emperor."

Lari paled as he stood next to Kial. "You always get the easy work and I get stuck with the hard jobs."

"That's because you're much more able to cope with them than me, Lari," responded Kial, a malicious twinkle in his eye. "Now sit down and report!"

Kial stood and pushed Lari down into the seat in front of the screen of the laservid.

Lari picked up the solid-state microphone and spoke into it. "Calling Ming XIII. Calling Ming XIII. Time probe aye dash seven, reporting in. Time probe aye, dash seven, from aye dash seven dee one two aitch, minus three aught one wye, three one seven dee, eighteen aitch, three seven em, one one ess."

Kial grinned. "Very good."

The laservid screen glowed a dull lavender. Then a face appeared in the lines of the screen. Lari cringed. It was a thin, ascetic, pinched face with a narrow jaw, a wide forehead, a widow's-peak skullcap, and slanted, piercing black eyes. The nose was thin and as vicious as a knife blade. A Mandarin-style mustache flowed down over the edges of the mouth, with an odd double-pointed Mephistophelian beard extended on past the trowel chin.

"Your Highness," Lari began stiffly, "we arrived here as scheduled in Time zone minus three aught one wye, three one seven—"

"I know all that, you idiot!" snapped a high-pitched voice on the laservid. "What happened?" The laservid audio began to whine.

"Your faithful agents, sire, immediately ascertained the presence of Flash Gordon on the superway to Arboria, as reported in the annals. Directing the antimatter neutralizer ray onto the suspension system of the jetcar he was driving, we blew it off the roadway."

"Get on with it!" screeched the face in the screen.

"However, sire, before we could tune our antimatter neutralizer force field to the special bone structure of Flash Gordon and the woman, he got out of—"

"In short, you bungling idiots, you've ruined everything, haven't you?" the sarcastic voice whined in the laservid audio.

Lari quailed. The purple face in the vidscreen seemed outraged.

"Do I have to tell you how to do everything?" Ming XIII asked ironically.

"Yes, Your Highness." Lari cringed. "I mean, no, Your Highness."

The face receded as Ming XIII seemed to back off a moment to think. Then the face appeared again.

"It's very simple. You've lost him now, but all you have to do is use your time belts!"

"Our time belts?" Lari's voice quavered.

"Yes, your time belts!" The face grew in size and the eyes seemed to pierce Lari's. "Set the digital chronometers back a few hours. Then all you have to do is steal Flash Gordon's weapons before you attack him."

"But Your Highness—how?"

"Get into that jetcar before he does! It's so simple, a moron could reason it out!"

Kial pushed Lari aside. "I understand, sire. We're to move back in time, steal Flash Gordon's weapons from the jetcar. Then he won't be able to come after us with his own—how was it described in the Annals of Time—oh, yes, blaster pistol."

"Right," said Ming XIII.

"But sire," Lari began in a trembling voice.

"What is it?" Ming XIII asked crisply, his burning eyes filling the screen.

"Where can we find the jetcar?"

Ming XIII's eyes narrowed. He turned and consulted a long strip of readout paper next to him. "Umm, yes. Here we are. Flash Gordon and Dale Arden arrived from Earth system at the spaceport in the forest the previous midnight. That's where they picked up the jetcar and that's where you're to steal those weapons!"

"Yes, Your Highness," said Kial, bowing before the vidscreen. "We'll fix him!"

"You'd better. Now get to it! You're wasting time."

Kial stared. "Well, sire, we can always retrieve lost time with our time belts, can't we?" He smiled.

"Idiot! Get moving, you two. You're not coming back here until you fix Flash Gordon, or I'll have you both met by the armed forces special squadron in Mingo Square. A fine pair of royal secret police you are!"

"Your Highness!"

"Bah!"

The screen went blank.

24

Kial turned and saw Lari looking at him, perspiration pouring down his face.

"All right, dummy," snapped Kial. "Let's get moving. You heard the emperor."

CHAPTER 5

In the special projects chamber of the Royal Palace of Mingo, the tall, gaunt, caped figure of Ming XIII paced back and forth over the royal carpet of synthofur. His thin saffron features were distinct in the brightly lighted laboratory; his black eyes glistened like ripe olives. His beard and mustache were stiffened by wax from the honeycombs of the forest kingdom's wild sassafras bees—which delicacy had been smuggled in over the borders by Ming's agents.

Emperor Ming paced to the window and gazed out onto the public square. Groups of royal police and palace courtiers mingled in small groups. The thrusting spires of the city of Mingo lay beyond, interlaced with the multi-tiered streets crawling with atom-powered mobiles and flight-belted pedestrians.

Ming smashed his right fist into his left palm and mouthed an oath. "Those stupid dolts! I'm surrounded by idiots and clods! How can we fight that rabble of the forest kingdom with only third-rate intellects and slaves programmed to stupidity?"

The door to the special projects chamber opened. Ming wheeled about quickly.

"Gorp!" he exclaimed. "Get over here instantly. I've got another report from the special agents on border patrol."

War Minister Gorp bowed and smiled sardonically. He was as slick and fleshy as Ming was gaunt and boned. His eyes were violet, a curious mutant strain caused by the blending of earthling blue and mongolite black. His hair was fair and worn long, in contrast to Ming's skullcap that made him appear completely bald. Gorp's long golden hair was tied in a purple bow in the back, a good twelve inches hanging down his back in piratical fashion.

He wore balloon sleeves, comparable to the military costume of Dynasty XIII, and balloon trousers tucked into crimson boots made of synthahide.

"Yes, sire," Gorp said as he came to stand by Ming. His violet eyes twinkled with some inner amusement.

Ming was annoyed. "You always remind me of a cat that's just finished off the cream jug. Will you go over to the battle board and look at it? You're war minister, not me, and if Arboria's troops wipe out our force at the border, I'll have your head mounted in Mingo Square!"

Gorp sauntered over to the battle table, a long trestle affair that ran half the length of the room. Over it was suspended a transparent sheet of old-fashioned plexiglass, interlined with a map of Mongo. Red circles and black circles had been affixed to the surface with quick-stick. "What is it that's disturbing you, sire?" Gorp asked in his liquid, half-laughing voice.

"I've got news from the border!" snapped Ming. "President Barin's troops are massing near Trento, a small river town. If the news is true, we're liable to be overrun and the main road to Mingo threatened!"

Gorp tapped his two front upper teeth with his forefinger as he considered.

"Are these agents your usual breed of liars and cheats, Emperor?" he asked.

Ming smashed his fist down on the battle board, making the pile of maps jump. "Don't you criticize my spies, Gorp! Your army-intelligence agents are no better! Riffraff, river rats, scavengers!"

"I'm certainly not criticizing," Gorp said mildly. "I am hoping only for a straight answer."

"They may be exaggerating," Ming admitted, "but it's better to be safe than sorry."

"An amusing comment," Gorp said. "It contains a grain of truth, like all clichés."

"What shall we do?" cried Ming.

Gorp stared closely at the transparent map. He traced

26

with a finger the great river, then the roadway between Arboria and the spaceport, and then over to Mingo City.

"The time-probe teams," Gorp murmured, "have they been successful?"

Ming's features twitched. "Partially."

"Partially?" Gorp repeated, his violet eyes afire with laughter. "Did all three fail?"

"Nothing failed yet!" snapped Ming defensively. "The primary probe team is standing by for the right moment to act. The secondary probe team is still on patrol, trying to carry out their objective."

"Which is?" Gorp prompted.

"It's Gordon," said Ming savagely. "Gordon and Arden! Our royal police can't seem to divert them."

Gorp nodded sardonically. "But that's the secondary phase, isn't it? What about the primary team?"

Ming bit his upper lip. "They're waiting. The minute Gordon is neutralized, they act."

"If-if-if," Gorp growled in a semblance of hopelessness. "*If* the primary probe team succeeds, and *if* the secondary probe team succeeds, *then* and only then can the tertiary probe team act and bring in the secret army of blue men to take Arboria!" Gorp suddenly chuckled. "It's a good plan, Emperor, turning back in time and wiping out Arboria and Prince Barin's forces so they can never make it into our century, but it won't work with the idiots you have in your royal police!"

Ming spun on Gorp, his face livid. "It's only a momentary setback, I tell you!"

Gorp threw back his head and laughed. "Setback? It's a catastrophe! Those fools. They couldn't even divert Flash Gordon and Dale Arden, could they? No, I thought not."

Ming strode along the battle table until he was face to face with his war minister. The corpulent man did not give ground one inch.

"It was a fiasco," Ming admitted in a hushed voice. "At least, up to this point it has been unsuccessful."

"I could have guessed," replied Gorp, sighing.

"But my agents are working on Gordon and Arden. We'll get them."

Gorp tapped his front teeth again as he gazed at the war map.

27

"Well, all I have to say is that it has to work, sire." He spoke with not a little sarcasm. "You've provoked a war you can't hope to win. And you've tried to use me as a scapegoat." Gorp's violet eyes were gleaming. "It's a risky business, Emperor. You can't cover up years and years of corruption here by staging a flashy war and taking the people's minds off their troubles."

"Now, see here—" Ming blurted out.

"Poverty. Inflation, with the mingot worth one-thousandth what it was ten years ago. Immorality rampant. A breakdown in the social structure. Vice. Perversion. Indecency. Murder. Riots." Gorp shook his head wearily, flicking at a spot of lint on his balloon sleeve. "I'm afraid you've bitten off more than you can chew, Ming."

Ming's saffron face turned red. *"Emperor!* you civilian! I am *Emperor Ming.* You address me as such. I am not a commoner like yourself. Not a halfbreed."

Gorp's smile vanished. His face hardened. "Sure, I'm half-earthling and half-mongolite. That's the difference between us. I'm only half-crazy. You're all crazy—if you think we can win this war with Barin."

"If we don't, you'll hang in Mingo Square!" cried Ming.

"I won't be alone," growled Gorp. "Half the community will be there with me. And if Barin and his constitutional democracy take over this archaic and rotten dictatorship, I wouldn't be surprised if Ming XIII leads all the rest."

"Enough of this haggling!" screamed Ming. "Get onto that war board and try to figure out some tactic to wipe out that force of Barin's."

Gorp pondered. "Where is that readout from the Annals of Time?"

Ming blinked. Then he moved over to a large bank of computers that lined a far wall of the chamber. "It was over here somewhere. You mean the one we used to dispatch those three time probes?"

"Right. Maybe we picked the wrong era."

Ming shook his head in self-pity. "I left it in your hands, Gorp. Maybe I should have done it myself."

Gorp ignored him. "Have you got it?"

Ming held out a roll of wide graph paper from a tight roll. Wiggly lines were imprinted on it in blue ink.

"Here it is."

Gorp unrolled the graph paper and spread it out on the trestle table. "Two hundred years ago. Two hundred and fifty. Three hundred. Minus three aught one. That's it, all right. Right here. It corresponds to the readout from the Annals of Time. It's the most vulnerable moment in Flash Gordon's celebrated life on Mongo. For our purposes, I mean. He's away from his protectors, that man Zarkov and Prince Barin. And Barin is sitting on a volcano and doesn't know it. Ming I has that secret army in the forest kingdom, just waiting for the right moment to ride in and take over. But with Gordon coming to Arboria from an extended trip to Earth, it will be completely out of our hands when they meet. We've simply got to keep them apart until"—Gorp narrowed his eyes—"until team three gets Barin."

"If only there were some way to proceed in case they don't stop Gordon," muttered Ming.

"No such luck," snorted Gorp. "Once Prince Barin celebrates the anniversary of the founding of the city, and once Gordon is decorated for his work on Mongo, then Barin will consolidate the forest kingdom. The forest kingdom is bound to become a constitutional democracy, as is written in the Annals of Time."

Gorp ran his fingers along the lines, glancing at the digital dates along the margin of the sheet. He shook his head in annoyance.

"The army of blue men," he muttered. "We've been unable to locate them in the readouts. Are you sure there isn't something wrong with the computers? A piece of lint in the electromagnetic circuitry, or something?"

"Absolutely not," said Ming. "It's been checked out by experts."

"Experts," said Gorp sorrowfully. "I don't like it. That army is right here in the records. Sent out by Ming I to infiltrate the forest kingdom and strike at Arboria. But there's no indication of what happened to it." Gorp sighed in dejection.

"There's nothing wrong with—" Ming began.

Gorp interrupted. "The Annals of Time has analyzed the data correctly. We've got to hit Barin there and we've got to divert Gordon from the hit or he's liable to foul it up." Gorp nodded. "We hit there, or never."

The violet eyes rested on Ming's features a moment, almost with contempt.

"It's so serious, Your Excellency, that if you don't trust the men on your time probes, you should do the job yourself."

Ming's face turned pallid. "Me? Go through time in that Tempendulum?"

Gorp's smile was underlaid with amusement. "Don't you trust the scientific geniuses who made it for you, sire?"

"Well," Ming XIII said, swallowing hard, "I'm sure the machine works. They did get there. But"—he swallowed again—"Gorp, you're a nuisance! Will you get out of here? I've got work to do! I want you to look over those battle plans again."

Gorp bowed at the waist, touching his forefinger to his forehead.

"Sire, I beg to withdraw."

Ming XIII saluted in return, his face stony.

The door slammed hard.

CHAPTER 6

The spaceport serving the forest kingdom was illuminated only by night lights as the figures of two men appeared in the darkness and walked toward the parking lot that lay outside the landing pads and control towers surrounding the airfield.

"Two hours after midnight," Kial whispered with a grin. "That was an easy trip, wasn't it?"

Lari shook his head, bewildered. He fingered the time-travel pack in his belt. "I don't get it, Kial. One minute it's the middle of the day, the sun in the sky. The next minute it's after midnight and we're here at the spaceport."

"Forget it," snapped Kial irritably. "Now where are

those jetcars? I remember Flash Gordon's was silver, wasn't it?"

"Right. It was a zarcar model. But how could it be here, Kial? It's wrecked on the superway to Arboria. We did it with the antimatter ray."

"Shut up!" snapped Kial. He pulled Lari back into the shadows of the girder span. "Look out—it's a guard. He's dressed in the forest-kingdom garb of hunter's green. At least, he looks like pictures I've seen in history vidtapes."

"History vidtapes," Lari repeated, dumbfounded. "What are you talking about, Kial?"

"It's three hundred years ago, dummy! The forest kingdom was in a state of almost medieval socioeconomic chaos. City folk. Woods folk. Rich. Poor. Archaic. Don't you know anything?"

"I only know it's cold and it's night and I don't know how it could be early morning after it's high noon."

Kial clapped his hand in exasperation over Lari's mouth. Lari attempted to speak, but no sound escaped.

The guard, a strapping man in a buckskin tunic tied on with thongs and a wide leather belt, green doublet, and soft knee-length boots, stood in the shadow of a large girder span exactly like the one behind which Kial and Lari were hidden.

"Who goes there?" he called out in a rough forest-kingdom dialect. "I can hear ye! Or is it only some wee forest animal?" There was a pause. "Aye!" The guard laughed. "Me ears must have been deceiving me. Not that it's unusual these crisp cold nights."

He peered into the darkness, shading his eyes a moment, and then shook his head.

"If ye're out there, make haste with ye, and don't think we won't catch ye if it's vandalism ye're after causing. Hear me?"

Kial struggled to keep Lari's mouth closed.

The guard finally turned and strode past the group of jetcars parked out under the stars and vanished into the main building of the spaceport.

"He looked to be a tough customer," said Kial, letting Lari's mouth go. "I'm glad he didn't catch us."

"Now what do we do?"

"We find Flash Gordon's car. It's silver with gold trim."

31

Kial scrutinized the jetcars and finally he reached around and grabbed Lari's arm. "Here it is," he whispered. "Now we've got to get the blaster pistols out of it."

"What are they?" Lari muttered. "Blaster pistols?"

"Come on, Lari! That's the kind of weapon they used in those ancient times. I think they came from Earth originally. Very inferior to our own molecular disintegrators, our antimatter neutralizers, and even our own neuro pistols that are the modern equivalent of the ancient stun guns."

"I don't know what you're talking about," Lari said miserably. "And I'm cold. Can't we get this over with?"

Kial opened the driver's door of the jetcar and searched the side pocket carefully.

"Here we are!" he cried triumphantly, and pulled out a blaster pistol. "Wait a minute—I thought he had his in a holster."

"He did," said Lari. "He wore it on his waist."

"But this one isn't in a holster."

"Maybe he put it in a holster later."

"Why would he keep a gun he was used to carrying in a holster in the side pocket of a car?" Kial was worried.

"Then if he carried it in a holster, maybe he's got it in the holster now."

Kial nodded. "That makes sense, Lari."

"Sure it makes sense," Lari said loudly.

"And that means we've got to go after him right now and find out if he has another blaster pistol in the holster, or if this is the only one he has."

"How's that again, Kial?"

"Forget it," snapped Kial. "Wait!" He leaned across the seat of the zarcar and fumbled in the console compartment. It was empty. He shook his head and slammed the door closed. "No holster."

"We've got one blaster pistol, haven't we?" Lari quavered. "Isn't that enough?"

"No!" snapped Kial. "If he's armed, he's dangerous. We've got to get that other blaster away from him." Kial's face hardened. "That is, if he has it."

"Kial," wailed Lari. "I'm all mixed up!"

"You were born mixed up," snapped Kial. He glared at him. "If you were born, which I'm beginning to doubt."

"What do you mean?" Lari whimpered.

"I mean we've got to get out of here and locate Flash Gordon fast!"

"How do we do that?"

"With our brains," Kial growled. He stood by the zarcar and frowned.

"Why don't we report in to Ming XIII," Lari said brightly. "He'll tell us what to do."

"Dummy! How do we report to him when we've got to get back to the Tempendulum to make contact?"

"Oh, yeah . . . well, we'd have to air-travel back on our belts."

"We haven't time," Kial replied irritably. He started walking through the jetcars in the lot. Across the way, he could see faint lights burning at a small construction site on the edge of the woods.

"Where are we going?" Lari asked, running to keep up with Kial's big strides.

"To the inn, dummy," replied Kial, pointing to the light glimmering against the backdrop of the trees. "If Flash Gordon's zarcar is ready and waiting for him, the chances are he's already landed from Earth. In that case, wouldn't he be staying overnight at the Spaceport Inn?"

"Yeah," said Lari, his eyes lighting up.

A few minutes later, they stood inside the entrance to the faintly lighted inn. A fire glowed cheerfully in the fireplace. A half-dozen tables with round wooden tops were crowded together in the room, with a short plank bar running along one wall. Thick rafters supported the wooden planks by a low cathedral ceiling.

The inn was deserted.

Kial shut the door. He and Lari stood there staring about, their eyes gradually becoming accustomed to the darkness.

"It's past midnight," whispered Lari. "That's why there's no one here."

"Right. But it's an inn. They're open all night. Somebody'll come."

"So we ask somebody, dummy!"

Lari nodded.

At that moment a door opened at the far end of the

33

bar, and a figure loomed in the darkness. The firelight danced over the figure of a young girl who apparently had just risen from bed. She was fastening a wrapper around her body with a belt. Under the wrapper she wore an old-fashioned chiton. The wrapper resembled a monk's cloak and hood. Her long hair hung down her back. She was pert and saucy.

"Aye?" she questioned in the forest-kingdom dialect. "How can I be helping ye?"

"We're looking for friends of ours," announced Kial, striding confidently forward.

"By the shade of King Barin! Who be ye? And whence have ye come dressed in that strange outlandish fashion?"

Kial blinked. He looked down at his clothing. "We're— we're—" He turned helplessly to Lari, who stared at him with wide, frightened eyes.

"I'll call the law," said the young woman as she advanced on them, reaching out and grabbing up a bottle of stout from the side of the bar. "Now get out of here with ye, do ye hear me?"

Kial held up his hands. "Please, miss! It's just that we're actors!" He gained confidence. "A traveling troupe of us is stranded at the spaceport, bumped from a flight to the Arcturus Galaxy."

The young woman stood very still, staring at Kial's face. He could see now that she was very pretty, with flaxen hair, light-blue eyes, and a round face with full lips. Her body was shapely inside the monk's robe.

"Bumped, is it?" she asked, looking at him carefully. Then her eyes took in Lari.

Lari blinked, trying to keep up with the fast-moving conversation. Actors? Bumped?

"My name's Kial," said Kial, waving Lari aside. "I'm originally from Mercury in the Earth Solar System."

"Aye. That accounts for the strangeness of yer accent, and the vacancy of yer features," said the girl in her woodsy accent. "All right. Me? I'm Magg, that's short for Margaret, from the forest kingdom it is, and proud of it!"

"This is Lari," said Kial, waving at his companion.

"Aye," Magg said. "Now what'll ye be needing, strangers to our forest kingdom? A mug of mead? A room? A bed?"

34

"Talk. Drink. Information." Kial smiled warily.

Magg continued to study him. Then she backed off and nodded quickly. "Sit ye down."

And she bustled off behind the bar where Kial heard her banging mugs and bottles together. Lari sat down next to him at the round wooden table.

Kial leaned over with his mouth close to Lari's ear. "You keep out of this, Lari. Leave it to me."

"Sure, Kial," Lari replied. "I'll leave it to you." He blinked. "What is it I'm leaving to you?"

"The wooing of the damsel," said Kial, his eyes dancing. "I'm going to worm out of her where Flash Gordon is. Take it from me—she knows."

"How do you know she knows?" Lari asked quickly.

"I don't know she knows, dummy," snapped Kial. "But I intend to find out!"

"But if she doesn't know, then she can't tell you, can she?"

"I tell you, she knows, Lari!"

"How do you know?"

"I don't know if she knows any more than you know if she knows," Kial snapped. "She's the only one who knows if she knows, but before I'm through, I'm going to know and you'll know, too, if she knows."

"How do you know?" asked Lari.

"I know because—" Kial stopped, fuming. "Leave the wench to me, Lari. No interference. You understand? You'll flummox the whole deal."

Lari nodded sadly.

Magg came up with the mugs of mead. She set them down with a bang. "Tell me," she said, eying Lari. "What play is it ye're touring the forest kingdom with?"

Lari's eyes got big. He opened his mouth to speak, but no sound came out.

"It's called *The Time Machine*," said Kial.

Magg frowned. "It's not been heard of around these parts. Are ye sure it's all that great?"

"It's very big on Mercury," Kial retorted. "That's why the Mercury Players are touring the galaxies with it."

Magg turned to Lari. "Lari," she said, the "r" sounding like a purr on her tongue, "would ye like another mug of mead?"

Lari opened his mouth again.

"Another round," said Kial, leaning forward.

Magg gathered up the empties and went behind the bar.

Kial turned to Lari. "Stop trying to butt in, dummy! I've got this girl almost sewed up. As soon as I get her to myself in a dark corner, you sneak into Flash Gordon's room and steal the blaster pistol."

"But, Kial, first we've got to find out where his room is," said Lari.

"I mean, after we find out where Gordon's room is," Kial said in exasperation.

Magg set down two steaming mugs of mead. She looked into Lari's face again.

"Them's strange clothes ye're wearing, ye ken? That's what made me wonder where ye'd come from."

Lari looked down at his garb and stammered, "It's of the very best material."

"Wearing the costume of the play saves the cleaning bills," said Kial with an ingratiating smile.

"I see," said Magg, still looking into Lari's eyes. "Ye've a very nice-looking face and I suppose that's why ye chose the stage, eh, Lari?"

Lari beamed. He started to speak.

"Truth of the matter is," Kial said, cutting in, "we're looking for two of our company that came this way."

Magg smiled at Lari.

"A man and a woman," said Kial, leaning forward and almost touching Magg's flaxen hair with his nose.

Lari smiled at Magg.

"Flash Gordon and Dale Arden," said Kial, poking his face in between Magg and Lari.

"Aye," said Magg, almost whispering. She reached out her hand and took hold of Lari's.

"Are they here in the inn?" Kial asked with annoyance.

"Aye," said Magg dreamily. The firelight flickered on her face. Kial looked at Lari and almost flew into a rage. "Snap out of it!"

"Aye," said Lari with a smile.

"What room?" Kial demanded loudly, reaching out and putting a firm clamp on Magg's shoulder.

"Room?" she repeated mistily. "Oh. Flash Gordon has the last room on the end. Dale Arden is in the one next to

36

that. I think they have a thing about each other." Magg giggled.

Kial nodded. "Lari," he said.

Lari and Magg were close together now, their chairs next to each other against the wall. Magg's arm was around Lari's neck and Lari's arms were around Magg's waist.

" 'Tis a beautiful man ye be," Magg sighed, closing her eyes.

Kial leaped to his feet. The chair went over backward behind him.

"Nincompoop!" he snapped. "I'll find the man myself!"

"And 'tis a beautiful girl ye be," Lari said. "Now isn't that a coincidence?"

He was speaking with a beautiful forest-kingdom accent.

And then neither said much of anything.

CHAPTER 7

In the darkened hallway of the Spaceport Inn, Kial gripped the large iron key ring in his hand and smiled grimly.

"It's a good thing I ordered Lari to distract that barmaid's attention. Once she was occupied with him, it was easy to take the key ring from her belt."

He moved slowly down the darkened hall.

"Last door on the end," he said musingly. "Let's see. Here we are." He squinted. "It's certainly dark here. And the smell! Whew! I don't see why these forest-kingdom types cling so scrupulously to their ancient woodsy traditions. Why, the smell alone would make me tear down all these ancient inns and put up some new modern clean-air buildings."

He inserted the third key in the lock after trying the first two. Number three fit.

"But I forget that it's three hundred years ago. People had a different idea of life-styles then. Too bad."

The door creaked open. Kial winced. "Sh!" he cautioned himself. Then he realized he was talking to himself. He pushed the key ring aside and moved into the room. The door closed creakingly behind him.

Kial closed it as slowly as he could to mute the noise.

There was a small window at one side of the room. A bit of Mongo's fifth moon cast dull orange light onto the forest outside, but not enough to see by. However, Kial did make out the shape of a bunk in the center of the room. And he heard steady breathing.

Gordon? he wondered. It's got to be him.

Kial moved stealthily across the room and looked down at the bunk. Yes. A long body lay sleeping under a fur coverlet. Kial frowned. He was after the holster with the blaster pistol in it.

Then his roving eye spotted it hanging on one of the bedposts; the holster was buckled to the belt and the blaster pistol was in the holster.

Kial crept toward it.

The bunk creaked.

Startled, Kial turned, halting in midstep.

Flash Gordon must have turned over in his sleep, he thought. No problem.

And he reached out for the holster. It felt heavy. Kial slipped holster and pistol off the bedpost, holding them in his hand. If I take the holster, Kial decided, he'll know something's wrong. He'll simply get another weapon. Kial frowned. He was stumped. He shook his head in dismay.

Wait, he thought again. I saw Gordon with the holster just after the jetcar crash. He didn't use the blaster pistol, but he had it in his hand. I'll leave the holster here and take the blaster pistol. Gordon will think he's got the pistol on him. Since I already saw him with the holster strapped on, I know he felt he had the gun. When he tries to use it on me, he won't have it.

Kial felt perspiration form on his brow.

But what if he suspects? What if he checks it out? Kial closed his eyes. I'm trying to remember how this works.

Let's see if I can recall what the scientists told us about time streams and a priori and a posteriori effects. "We go back in time. We change something in the past. Everything that has happened in the future of that time cannot be altered. But a new branch of time is created, flowing parallel with the first. Therefore, at the moment I take this blaster pistol from the holster, I create a double time flow. One of the flows ends at the time the pistol is put to use. Then the second time flow becomes the true one. The one that went before is wiped out of the Annals of Time.

Kial was so nervous that he trembled.

I take the blaster pistol, but I leave the holster. When Gordon tries to use the blaster pistol, it will not be there, because I will have it when I reenter the true time flow.

He shook his head.

Scientists! I wish they'd never invented that stupid time machine.

Kial slipped the blaster pistol into his air-travel belt. He put the holster over the bedpost, then suddenly he was grabbed from behind. One arm was twisted up behind his back and the other held in a grip of iron.

"Sneak thief, eh?" a voice growled in his ear.

Flash Gordon!

"How did you get out of that bunk?" Kial asked hoarsely.

"How did you get into my room?" Flash asked.

Kial slammed his knee into Flash Gordon's thigh. Flash backed away momentarily and Kial ran for the doorway.

At least, he thought he ran for the doorway. In actuality, he ran toward a small window set in the back wall of the inn.

"Stop!" yelled Flash.

Terrified, Kial thrust his hands out in front of him to open the door, but encountered only air. The window of the room was open.

Kial felt himself suddenly tripped at mid-thigh by the windowsill and propelled forward. Head-first, he dove out through the open window and into the dark night.

Behind him, in the room he had left so quickly and so unexpectedly, Kial heard a sudden commotion. Voices from nearby rooms joined with that of Flash Gordon.

He had no time to think about that.

Like all heavily falling objects, Kial landed abruptly.

A moment later he blinked and tried to open his eyes. He was not really hurt, only stunned. He had landed in some kind of substance, a substance contained in a large receptacle of unseen dimension in back of the inn.

"Ugh!" he cried as he floundered in the oozy viscid matter. He wiped the stuff out of his eyes and realized that he was up to his neck in it. The slop pit of the Spaceport Inn lay directly underneath the room in which Flash Gordon had taken lodging for the night.

Lari and Magg heard the first cry together in the serving room of the inn.

"What's that?" Lari asked, sitting up.

"Who cares?" Magg asked sighing. "Oh, Lari!"

A moment later there were more shouts. Lari sat up again.

"Magg. It's my friend Kial."

"He can take care of himself." Magg's arms crept around his neck.

A scream sounded. To Lari, it seemed to be Kial's voice. He rose abruptly.

Magg was at his side, frowning. "I thought ye said he was a friend of Flash Gordon's."

"He said he was a friend of Gordon's," Lari reminded her.

"Just who be ye?" Magg asked, her face angry.

"I'm Lari and you're Magg."

"Silence to ye," snapped Magg. "If there's trouble at the inn because of ye—"

A door slammed upstairs. "He's escaped!" a woman's voice cried out.

"I'll get him!" roared the voice of Flash Gordon.

Magg reached out and pulled an enormous copper pot from the wall of the inn near the kitchen. "Ye're not a friend of Mr. Gordon's. Ye're a plain ordinary thief."

"Magg!" cried Lari. He put his hands over his head to protect it.

She swung the pot and it clanged loudly as it smashed into his skull. He ran for the first door he saw—the entrance to the kitchen.

Magg got in two more shots before he made it to the

door and pushed it open. It was night outside, but the moon of Mongo lit the sky faintly with a low-keyed glow.

In that orange glow, Lari could see a strange misshapen phantom in front of him, a being that seemed to rise from a murky, sticky mass of matter which adhered to it in gobs and chunks.

"Who is it?" Lari cried, halting.

Clang! Magg's aim was very good. She improved with practice. Lari stumbled and began running again.

"Lari?" Kial's voice was close to his ear.

Lari did not understand. The phantom was Kial, that he knew. But Kial was talking through a mouthful of mush.

"What?"

"Run!" gurgled Kial.

Lari bolted for the forest. And the girl with the pot ran right behind him.

A voice cried from a window of the inn. "Don't let them get away!"

"I won't," Magg promised.

But unfortunately, she did.

Exactly five minutes later in the woods behind the inn, Kial and Lari huddled behind an enormous sword fern.

"Did we shake them?" Kial wondered.

"I think so," Lari replied.

"Good. I don't mind saying I thought we were done for."

"Did you get the blaster pistol?"

"Yes. No thanks to you," growled Kial ill-naturedly. He turned the luca ring on his pinky and suffused the area around his hands with artificial light. They would both see the blaster pistol clearly.

The weapon had the letters "F.G.C.U.S.A." inscribed across the side of the barrel.

"Flash Gordon," Kial translated, pointing to the initials. "Colonel. That's right. The Annals of Time readout specified that he was a colonel by rank in the World Council." Kial mused. "United States of America. That's a political division on Earth. It was Flash Gordon's point of origin."

"Then that's the weapon he had when we found him on the superway." Lari frowned. "I mean when we *will* find him on the superway."

41

"Right. I remember he fumbled at the jetcar door pocket before he climbed out after the wreck. You recall?"

"I suppose so, but I thought he wore it in a holster around his waist."

"I left the holster there so he'd think he was armed."

Lari nodded. Then he sniffed the air. "Hey, Kial. What's that awful smell? You?"

"I don't care to discuss it," responded Kial.

"You know, that inn girl, Magg, guessed that we were thieves."

"Better thieves than royal police from Ming XIII," said Kial with a sigh.

"Did Gordon see you?"

"Of course he saw me, but it doesn't matter. We'll fix him as soon as we get back to the superway."

Lari got up and started walking.

"Dummy," snapped Kial. "Come back here."

Lari turned, puzzled.

"We don't walk! We go by time-travel."

"Oh," said Lari.

"Set your time-travel pack to ... let's see." Kial closed his eyes. "Plus seven aitch one five em three aught ess. And your space-travel pack to Mongo grid coordinates Latt plus one two seven degrees, two hours, five minutes, three seven seconds, and eight milliseconds; long plus eight aught degrees, five hours, five seven minutes, two seconds and one aught five milliseconds. Right?"

"You tell me, Kial," said Lari.

"I am telling you, dummy!" yelled Kial.

They set the digital readouts on their belts together.

And then both vanished.

CHAPTER 8

Flash studied the forest growth and the terrain briefly, and then turned to Dale.

"The origin of that ray is around here somewhere, but we haven't really got the time to search it out now. Not with those two at large. Let's get back to the jetcar."

"It won't do us any good," Dale said grimly. "It's obvious you can't fix the car. Do you think we can get a ride on the superway?"

"I have no idea," Flash answered thoughtfully. "I just don't like what's going on around here. I'm armed." He patted the holster at his waist. "But I want you to have a weapon, too. I've got an extra blaster pistol in the car. I always carry one spare." Flash peered grimly into the shadows behind the lavender-and-orange foliage. "I have a strange feeling that we haven't seen the last of that disintegrator ray or the two men who operated it."

"So have I," said Dale, shivering.

Together they walked through the scrub brush toward the wreckage by the superway. A scarlet alardactyl wheeled into view and then spun out of sight in the mustard sky.

"The birds are returning. I think our guests have departed," said Flash with a faint grin.

"But they might come back."

"You can be sure they will," Flash observed.

"What do they want?"

"Us."

"Why us?"

"That's for them to know and for us to find out," Flash said playfully.

Dale smiled. "It can't be any of Prince Barin's people."

"Dressed in that weird garb?" Flash snorted. "Not on

43

your life! They don't look like your ordinary Mingo type, either."

"I'd say they came from some other environment entirely," Dale replied.

"From another planet in the Mongo System?"

"Perhaps."

"Why attack us then?"

"And why disappear before our eyes!" Dale wrapped her arms around her chest, hugging herself. "It's spooky. I'm beginning to believe in witchcraft."

"There's got to be some scientific explanation," Flash insisted.

They came to the wreck of the jetcar by the side of the superway. Flash climbed in, opened the driver's door, and fumbled in the side pocket for his spare blaster pistol.

"It's gone," he said, looking up in surprise.

"What's gone?"

"The spare blaster."

"Are you sure? Maybe you left it in the console compartment instead."

Flash leaned over and opened the compartment on the dash. It, too, was empty.

"Not there, either."

Dale looked around uneasily. "It's getting spookier and spookier."

"I don't like it one bit," Flash said grimly. "Dale, you said the laserphone was out?"

"Yes."

"There's got to be some way we can signal Arboria and get in touch with Prince Barin. Maybe he'll have some clue to this strange business."

"I think we're going to have to walk the whole distance to Arboria."

Flash shrugged. "We can't be too many mongometers from the city. We were due to arrive in fifteen minutes. At our ground speed of 1,700 mongometers per minute, I'd guess about 25,000 mongometers, give or take a few."

"Flash, I can never remember how long a mongometer is."

Flash laughed. "Well, a mongometer is just about half the size of an earthmeter, and is measured in the same manner. One ten-millionth of the distance from the equator to the pole, measured along a meridian. Since Mongo's diameter is exactly half of Earth's, that cuts the circumference in half, too."

"Flash! You're beginning to sound just like Dr. Zarkov! How long is a mongometer? In feet?"

"Just over a foot and a half. Eighteen, nineteen inches."

"How many miles to Arboria?"

"Well, maybe six or seven miles." Flash frowned. "Beginning to sound like Zarkov, huh?"

Dale laughed.

"If we're going to walk, I'd better make sure my blaster pistol is in working order. I had some trouble with the firing pin last time I used it."

Flash unbuckled his holster and reached inside. He removed the blaster pistol without looking down at his hand, and then glanced at it.

His hand was empty.

He had felt the weapon. But now it was not in his hand.

"You should see the expression on your face!" Dale said, chuckling.

Flash stared at her. "What?"

"I mean, you look as if you'd seen a ghost!"

Flash looked down at his empty hand. "It's gone, Dale."

"What's gone?"

"My blaster pistol."

"But you said you had it in your holster."

"Dale, I took it out of the holster, and was just looking down at it to check the pin. It disappeared, but I felt it." Flash closed his eyes. "Maybe it was autosuggestion."

Dale stared. "You're just imagining it, Flash. It's all this talk about witchcraft and magic."

"No," said Flash. "I had it in my hand. And it's gone."

Dale looked around at the ground near the wreck. "You dropped it. That's all." Her voice rose.

"I had it and it vanished," snapped Flash. He looked around once more at the forest that surrounded them, with its paleozoic plants frozen in time, the weird lavenders and purples and oranges from Mongo's soil content. "I can feel someone out there, watching us."

"The first blaster pistol stolen from the car. The second stolen from your hand." Dale shivered again.

"Come on," demanded Flash. "The sooner we get out of here, the better I'll like it!"

"But where—?"

"To Arboria. Shank's mare."

Dale looked around once more at the suddenly unfriendly forest and hurriedly caught up with Flash. They walked rapidly over the weed-covered terrain to the lip of the superway. In a moment they were striding along the smooth surface of the pavement. In Mongo's lower gravitational pull, their steps were a bit longer than an average Earth step.

A sound in the forest off to the left brought Dale up short.

"What's that?"

Flash halted beside her on the superway, frowning. "I don't know."

The sound in the forest came again, exactly as it had come the first time. Now Flash recognized it as a high-pitched, screeching resonance, entirely inhuman.

"It's not a person, but it almost sounds like someone having hysterics," said Dale in hushed tones. "I mean, hysterics from laughter."

Flash glanced uneasily up and down the superway. "I don't like this being without any weapon." He sighed. He stared into the forest along the way. The superway wound through a stand of enormous lycopods, over two hundred feet in height. A lycopod was an evergreen mosslike herb. It had creeping stems, small, scaly leaves, and club-shaped candles. This particular variety resembled a ground pine, in Earth nomenclature.

Now an air-shaking crash reverberated inside the foliage, as if some enormous, massive, bounding creature were smashing trees and brush in its flight through the woods.

"There's something coming at us!" cried Dale.

Flash glanced around. There was a large round boulder behind a giant fern on the right side of the superway. "Take cover," he told her, pointing.

Dale ran across the superway and crouched down behind the rock.

"Come on!" she called to Flash.

Reluctantly Flash followed, glancing back over his shoulder at the stand of ground pines. He saw the needles and branches of the trees shaking as the weight of the unseen thing crashed through the foliage.

Flash crouched beside Dale. "Maybe that's what wrecked the jetcar," she said softly.

"No," said Flash. "The sound of that ray was different."

Dale shrugged.

"This is one of the forest kingdom's arrested species, I'll bet," Flash muttered. "It's too heavy for a salamander—we've had trouble with them before—and it doesn't sound like one of the rogue rodents. We'll have to wait for it to pass."

"If it doesn't smell us out, that is."

"I thought Zarkov had promised Prince Barin to clean out the timber around Arboria! It's still not safe to walk a mile outside the city walls. Last time I saw Doc he was working on a spray that would turn them all into docile cattle—salamanders, giant spiders, the aphids, and the killer beetles. Guess the formulation didn't work.

The giant lycopods began progressing slowly across the superway. Flash peeped over the edge of the boulder and suddenly saw an enormous and hulking mass press through a curtain of wavering club moss and squeeze out into the clearing by the superway.

Dale stifled a shriek.

Flash gripped her shoulder hard.

The creature was a hulking, eight-foot-high magnified version of an aphis-type insect of some kind, composed of a gelatinous substance that gave off a violet iridescence. As it stood there, its shape altered slightly, and Flash saw that it resembled an ordinary aphid, greatly enlarged.

"It's an aphid," whispered Flash. "I've heard about these murderous things. They don't subsist totally on vegetation, either. They like people."

"Good Lord!" exclaimed Dale.

The iridescent purple aphid extended the head of its body from the thorax and seemed to study the forest. Finally, its gaze centered on the boulder behind which Flash and Dale crouched.

It opened its mouth and a hideous screech echoed

through the forest, a screech that approximated, as Dale had said, the laughter of an hysterical woman.

"I never heard them mention the laughing aphid," Flash whispered. "But that's what it is."

"Maybe it's another mutant," murmured Dale. "I tell you, I don't like this primeval forest. I don't see why Prince Barin lets it exist this way."

"It's his ecology minister who's behind it. He wants to keep it primitive as a kind of nature preserve. Besides, they can't level the forest. They need the wood, Dale, not only for their city, but for everything they make. Even their clothing is fabricated from reconstructed wood fibers, you know."

Dale frowned. "Well, I don't like it one bit. Flash, the thing is staring right at us."

"If those are eyes, I guess you're right," said Flash.

Indeed, the laughing aphid was looking at them. It seemed to arch its body and get its long spiky legs moving, propelling its massive, purple, gelatinous body toward them.

They smelled a musty odor emanating from the giant aphid. It was the smell of old swamps, moldy figs, and human waste.

Flash gripped Dale's upper arm and lifted her quickly to her feet. "Run. Into the forest. It's our only chance. The thing is going to attack!"

"Attack? How?" Dale asked.

Flash shook his head. "I don't know. I wish I had my blaster pistol!"

"You haven't, so don't waste your time."

They were both on their feet and running for the club moss stand to their rear. The giant aphid stood in the middle of the superway; its gelatinous head rose, its eyes moved, and then it thrust its head forward and its enormous almost unseen mouth opened. A purplish quivering flame lashed out from the oral opening.

Flash experienced instant paralysis.

Dale was frozen beside him.

An enormous glob of sticky purple sputum had flashed out of the aphid's shapeless mouth—a glob as large as Flash was tall—and it had fallen on the two of them, trapping and paralyzing them where they stood.

48

Flash could not move his arms. He could not breathe. He could not move his feet.

Through the jellied purple substance that surrounded him from head to foot, he saw that Dale, too, was imprisoned, unable to move. Together they stared helplessly at the giant aphid.

The aphid screeched its battle cry and the forest echoed with the sound of maniacal laughter.

Flash could feel the purple jelly tighten around him, squeeze in on him, press the air from his chest, and press on his ribs. Everything seemed to congeal around him. He experienced total suspension of all life functions.

CHAPTER 9

High in the treetop city of Arboria stood the spacious palace of Prince Barin, ruler of the entire forest kingdom. Inside the throne room a tall, black-haired man with a thick black beard raged up and down the lengthy celluloceram floor.

"All right, then, where are they? They should have been here a half hour ago!" he cried, flinging his long arms into the air.

"Calm down, Zarkov," said the man who stood with him in the middle of the large chamber. "You're always asking for trouble."

"I don't ask for it, Prince Barin," snapped Zarkov. "But I always get it!"

Dr. Zarkov was dressed in his usual high-buttoned laboratory robe, which he habitually wore both for scientific work as well as exploratory work.

In contrast, Prince Barin, ruler of the forest kingdom of Mongo, was attired in a three-piece sumptuously rich full-dress regalia fit for receptions, formal affairs, and other kingly functions. His mantle was trimmed in rich gold-

and-green embroidery, with a tunic of crimson and trousers of silver. He was shorter than Zarkov, but stood very straight. His black hair was crew-cut in an old-fashioned Earth manner.

"I just talked with my traffic minister, Zarkov," Prince Barin continued. "He assures me there is no trouble of any kind on the superway through the forest."

"You should have let me clean out that area last month when I finalized that neurogas formula I made for the pig men of Pogoland. I could have wiped the place clean of all potential danger. If Flash and Dale have fallen into the hands of the golden ants or the salamanders, I'll never forgive you."

"Defoliation is not our way here in the forest kingdom, Zarkov," Prince Barin replied patiently. "We just don't believe in that kind of thing."

"You'd rather have anyone who drives through that section take his life into his hands—is that it?" demanded Zarkov, his flesh turning slightly pink.

"Come now, Zarkov." Prince Barin smiled. "I don't think anything has happened to them."

"Then where are they? We know they left the spaceport over five hours ago! Why you have to keep this city so damned isolated is beyond me!"

"Roads were invented by generals bent on conquest," Prince Barin reminded Zarkov. "Keeping ourselves isolated here has saved us time and again from the depredations of Ming the Merciless and his armies."

"The spaceport could have been built closer to the capital," said Zarkov, grumbling. "I tried to construct one on the slopes overlooking the city, but your minister of ecology voted me down."

"And well he might," Prince Barin responded. "You'd have us ripping out trees to clear airfields, polluting the air with burning wood, and ruining the water table throughout the kingdom. We'd be a desert, Zarkov, a desert!"

"Better a desert than a tangled wasteland," muttered Zarkov, "crawling with all kinds of goblins and beasties." There was a pause. "Besides, I still maintain that a forest is the perfect place for an invading army to hide out. You're too decent a person, Prince Barin, to believe in all the evil things that lie in wait out there around you. It's the good who wind up paying for the bad."

Prince Barin laughed heartily. "You're really testy today, Zarkov. I don't know what's got into you."

Zarkov slammed his fist into one of the plyoform chairs. "I'm worried about Flash and Dale. It just isn't like them to be late."

"We could set out on the superway and meet them," Prince Barin suggested.

Zarkov shook his head. "It would take too long."

"Then how can we help find them?"

"The airscout," said Zarkov.

"Not the new one," Prince Barin replied nervously.

"Why not?"

"It hasn't passed its emission tests yet. And you haven't flown it, either."

"Listen, when I design a new rocket, it stays designed!" barked Zarkov. "You think we have to go through those tests all the time? Not with Zarkov's solid-state circuitry! I've got that flailing problem licked, I tell you. Just because the prototype went down into the Sea of Kyrile——"

"Putting three of my best scientists in the hospital for months on end," interrupted Prince Barin.

"——doesn't mean it's going to crack up this time! Besides, this airscout is a one-man affair. It can't go wrong."

Prince Barin waved his hand despairingly. "Take it then. I see you're bent on looking for Flash and Dale—and good luck to you."

Zarkov sulked. "I don't think your heart's in this, Prince Barin."

"Zarkov, what do you want from me? Hymns? Best wishes? Soft soap? I can give you anything. I agree that you should try to find them. There. Is that better?"

Zarkov brightened. "I'll check the stations along the superway again. Then, if there's no news of them, I'll take up the airscout." His eyes gleamed. "You want to come along?"

Prince Barin blanched. "Next time, Zarkov. Next time perhaps."

Zarkov shrugged. "Well, I know you've got to prepare the palace and the public square for the anniversary celebration of Mongo's liberation from the tryanny of Ming

51

the Merciless. I don't want to tire you out with my little scouting expedition."

The door at the far end of the throne room opened abruptly. Prince Barin turned from the center of the room and beckoned to the man in the door.

"Approach, Minister."

Zarkov watched the stolid, muscular minister of intelligence approach. Hamf was a bleak, gray-eyed man with absolutely no expression and an enormous bald forehead. He seemed to have no eyebrows. All there was of him seemed caged in the bulbous skull above the small, pinched, chinless face.

"Thank you, Your Excellency."

"Well?" Prince Barin looked over his shoulder at Hamf as he came up to him.

"Sire," said Hamf, glancing at Zarkov covertly, "I have a confidential report."

"Zarkov won't leak it," Prince Barin said confidently. "Speak up."

"Yes, sire," Hamf said nervously. "We have intercepted a message from Mingo to an outpost near the Mingo-Arboria border."

"Is it important?" asked Prince Barin. "You always bring these notes to me. I like to read the ones dealing with the spicy amours of Mingo's minions, but I'm tired of hearing about the latest military appropriations at their palace."

"This is a bit more important, sire," said Hamf. "We've translated a code message and interpreted it. Sire, a force of undesirables is building up on the Mingo-Arboria border near Outpost Daj."

Zarkov glowered. "Undesirables?" he boomed out. "What does that mean? Have they got chicken pox? Mumps? Poison ivy?"

Hamf gave Zarkov a withering glare. "It's a euphemism for enemy troops, Dr. Zackov."

"It's Zarkov, and don't you forget it," snapped Zarkov. "Enemy troops, eh?" He turned to Prince Barin. "Do you believe this?"

Prince Barin rubbed his chin slowly. "I'm inclined to be skeptical. We've had no other hint at all of activity in that

52

region. I'm going to think it over, Hamf. Thank you very much."

Hamf glanced from Prince Barin to Zarkov and started to back away. "Yes, sire."

"I believe it," Zarkov said suddenly, eying Prince Barin. "You're too optimistic, Prince Barin, about people. I never will understand you. You don't trust machinery at all, but you trust people. Me, I'm the opposite. I don't trust people as far as I can throw them. But I do trust machinery. Now, what kind of a madman is it who trusts Mingolites?"

Prince Barin flushed. "You're calling me a fool, Zarkov?"

"Not a fool. An optimist. A thin line separates the two." Zarkov wheeled on Hamf. "Who are these undesirables, Hamf?"

Hamf's tiny mouth pursed. "We don't really know, Dr. Zackov. We've kept tabs on all of Ming's state troops. This is apparently a new division. We don't know where it comes from. Nor do we know who heads it up."

"That's important?" asked Zarkov.

"Yes. Because we know where every one of Ming's generals is stationed right now. If this force is preparing for an assault, we'd like to know who heads it. Then we could analyze its *modus operandi*."

Zarkov nodded. "Got you. You get back to central intelligence and keep on the laserphone, Hamf. Prince Barin wants you to concentrate on that report and find out if there's even a glimmer of truth in it. Ming would try to throw the capital in an uproar on a day set aside for a celebration like this one, wouldn't he?"

Hamf nodded sadly.

"Now get moving," snapped Zarkov.

Hamf left the throne room.

Prince Barin shook his head. "Zarkov, you're something else again. Why do you think this piece of intelligence is accurate?"

"Obviously that something is keeping Flash and Dale out there in the forest."

"You mean you think they've stumbled across that concentration of unknown troops? Is that it?"

"How can I know for sure?" Zarkov yelled, striding up and down furiously, flailing his arms in the air and making the celluloceram floor shake with the tread of his boots. "It's a possibility, anyway."

"The minute you see anything out of the ordinary, call me by ship's laserphone." Prince Barin watched Zarkov alertly.

Zarkov halted, face to face with the prince.

"Right, then," he said, made an about-face, and bounded across the throne room to the door.

All Arboria lay below him as he rose in the airscout through the immense oaks and larches that grew around the forest kingdom's capital. Zarkov looked down once and saw the palace pass by beneath him.

He pressed the retrorocket activator, jockeyed the controls, set the course computer for point between the spaceport-Arboria superway and the Mingo-Arboria border, and leaned back in the plyoform seat, arms folded across his broad chest.

"It's doing beautifully," he said to himself, scanning the dials and digital readout ports that cluttered the console in front of him. "I'm glad I simplified the design of the board. It's maddening to have to read fifty-two dials all at once; forty-five isn't so bad at all."

The airscout mounted the heavens, heading in a direction away from Arboria. The last Zarkov saw of the city was the spire of the House of Meditation as it vanished to the rear of the city.

The dense primeval forest of Mongo stretched out far below him.

Zarkov picked up the laserphone, punched out the call numbers of the spaceport, and was immediately in touch with the spaceport commissioner.

"Any news of Flash Gordon?" Zarkov boomed out.

"Nay, sire," said the voice of the commissioner. "But then, there isn't much traffic today. Holiday and all that."

"Roger," said Zarkov, remembering his flyboy days in England on Earth.

The airscout passed over the thin winding thread that was the superway. Zarkov flicked the switch to manual control and took the wheel in his hands. He watched through the bubbleglass and followed the thin white line through the jungle around it.

He could see nothing at all.

"Calling zee five six, zee five six," a voice said on the laserphone.

Zarkov lifted the laserphone. "Zarkov."

"Report from the border," said the voice of Hamf. "My agent found a corpse in the woods. Dead for several hours. One of our agents. Vanished two years ago. He'd been"—Hamf choked—"he'd been surgically debrained, Zarkov. Total massive frontal lobotomy. Evidence of electrode implants in his skull."

Zarkov swallowed. "Good god, Hamf!"

"Something's out there, Zarkov. Something evil."

"I'll find it," Zarkov promised.

He hung up the laserphone.

A sudden tremor made the airscout buck slightly in the air. Zarkov glanced at the dials. The needles were all bouncing, the digital numbers flying around in a mad whirl.

Zarkov gripped the wheel, trying to steady the airscout.

"What's going on?" he muttered.

The airscout lurched and descended rapidly.

It was hurtling down on its side like a dead thing.

Zarkov fought the wheel. The flailing syndrome!

No response.

Tiny yellow puffs of smoke curled out of the end of the console. Zarkov could smell burning plyoplast.

The hydrogen fission cell must be out of control! If it burned through the lead sheathe, he'd be radiated.

The airscout turned over on its back, as if sensing its own imminent death.

Zarkov slammed against the ceiling. The airscout flipped back again. Then, with a tremendous crash, it hit.

CHAPTER 10

"Well, here we are," said Kial, "but where are we?"

Lari shook his head. "Don't ask me, Kial."

"I'm not, stupid! I'm just saying it."

"Then say what you mean," Lari retorted.

They were in a part of the forest kingdom that resembled every other part. There were primitive palm trees, giant cinnamon ferns, arrested conifers, and strange creeping vines that twisted among all the other growth.

"Where's the superway?" Lari asked suddenly.

"Dummy, that's what I've been trying to figure out for five minutes."

They had come through time and space as soon as they had activated their belt packs. However, in their haste to remove themselves from the vicinity of the Spaceport Inn, Kial had apparently miscalculated slightly either on their timing or on their siting. Whatever, they were now in a part of the forest kingdom that did not remotely resemble any part that they had seen before.

"Can't we get back to the Tempendulum by setting our time packs?" Lari asked tremulously.

"No! We'd get back to the proper time, but we'd be no nearer the Tempendulum. I marked my digital grids correctly. Something has probably gone wrong with the space pack. It's off."

"What do we do now?" Lari asked timidly.

"How do I know?" Kial asked growlingly.

"You're supposed to know. You're smarter."

"Who says?"

"You always say."

"Then it's true." Kial shook his head. "Well, we could always walk in a straight line. Eventually we'd cross the superway." He snapped his fingers as his eyes lighted up. "That's it?"

"What? Walk forever?"

"No! We described a straight line across the forest kingdom from east to west. Since the superway from the spaceport to Arboria proper runs north and south, we're bound to intersect the superway somewhere."

"But how do we do it without walking?"

"With our space-travel packs, dummy. Now, look, we'll set our grids to a point one mile to the east of us. We make that flight, check out the area, and then go another mile east."

"But what if the superway lies to the west?"

"When we get to the end of the forest, we'll come back, dummy."

"It seems—"

"Set your grids, and shut up!"

They found the superway in thirty-five minutes. In the middle of the pavement, they looked up and down and wondered exactly where they were in relation to Flash and Dale.

"Well," said Kial decisively, "let's go south. Then, if we don't find the wrecked jetcar, we'll come back the other way."

"All right," said Lari. "I'm tired, though, Kial. Have you got anything to eat or drink?"

"You should have filled up on steaming mead last night instead of all that hanky-panky," snorted Kial. "I've got a kelp energy bar, if you're interested."

"I'd eat anything," said Lari. "Even an algae sand on rye."

They munched on the kelp energy bars and then began the hopscotching pattern down the superway.

Suddenly Kial held up his hand. "Shh!"

"What is it?" Lari asked softly.

"Quiet! I can't hear if you talk."

"Why didn't you tell me not to, then?"

They listened.

Trees seemed to be crashing to the ground in the distance. There was a great deal of shuddering of the earth's surface under the superway. Then there was an ominous silence.

"What made that noise?" Lari asked, his face covered with perspiration.

57

"How do I know?" snapped Kial. "But we've got to find out."

"I make it on a direct line south," Lari said nervously, glancing at his digital grid setting.

"Me too," said Kial. "Let's go."

They activated the space packs and faded in on a stretch of superway some distance away.

"Look!" cried Lari.

"I see it," Kial muttered between clenched teeth. "Come on. Get out that blaster pistol you took from the jetcar. I've got Flash Gordon's."

They moved cautiously down the superway.

In the distance a purple iridescent creature that resembled a giant aphid stood in the middle of the superway and watched them approach.

"It's some kind of insect from Mongo's past," explained Kial.

"What kind?" Lari wanted to know.

"I'm no biologist," Kial retorted.

Lari halted.

Kial halted.

"It's watching us," Lari said. "Now it's moving toward us, Kial!"

"Get your blaster pistol ready, dummy," Kial said impatiently. "We'll both take him simultaneously." Kial shook with anxiety and fear.

The purple monster's eyes were focused directly on Kial and Lari. Suddenly it hunched forward and glided over the superway toward them. As it moved it exuded a glistening web of purple spoor. It moved quite rapidly.

Lari's hand trembled as he lifted the blaster pistol and pointed it at the enormous insect. Suddenly he cried out, "Kial! By the side of the superway. It's—it's Flash Gordon and Dale Arden!"

Kial stared past the advancing purple aphid. He could see the two human beings frozen in a large blob of purple jelly.

"By the orange moon of Mongo!" gulped Kial. "I don't believe it! This monster must have frozen them into eternity."

"Then we can go home. Flash Gordon is dead and we're safe at last."

58

Kial shook from head to foot. "Hold it, dummy! We don't know that for sure." He swallowed hard. "Maybe it's a trick."

"What trick?" Lari yelped. "Let's set our time packs, hit the Tempendulum, and get back to Ming XIII."

The purple aphid was rapidly closing the distance between them.

"Fire, dummy!" screamed Kial. "We've got to do this thing in, no matter what."

"Oh, yeah," said Lari, and squeezed the grip of the blaster.

The ray missed the monster and disintegrated a stand of club moss. By the time Lari had compensated for this angle of fire, Kial's ray was focused on the purple monster.

There was a high-pitched screech that offended Kial's ears, and the purple creature froze in its tracks on the superway and stared in astonishment at the blaster pistol in Kial's hands.

Lari's ray centered on the creature's chest? Neck? Head? Thorax?

"Keep firing!" cried Kial.

Slowly the purple monster swelled and swelled, like an overinflated balloon.

"It's getting bigger," cried Kial. "What can we do? It's apparently feeding on the energy from the blaster pistol."

Lari's face was white. "Kial, I can't turn the blaster off. It's eating up the ray. It's keeping me from turning it off!"

The high-pitched screaming laughter erupted again, louder this time, making the air reverberate.

"Let's get out of here," Kial screamed and turned to run.

Lari fought for control of the blaster pistol, which seemed to be controlled by the giant aphid. He could not move the blaster at all. The purple creature swayed toward him, hovered over him, looked directly at him.

Lari could hear Kial crash through the undergrowth, small sounds of utter despair issuing from his throat.

Lari watched the purple monster in front of him, his eyes bulging from their sockets.

Then the aphid thrust forward its head on its neck, its offensive oral cavity opened, and a gelatinous blob of purple jelly spewed forth toward him.

The gelatinous spittle touched him.

Lari recoiled, turned, and ran.

The jellied substance ran over him and covered him as he froze in his tracks.

He could not move.

The jellied effluence pressed in on him, crushing the breath out of his body.

The forest turned purple around him.

CHAPTER 11

In the dull glow that illuminated the inside of the airscout, Zarkov saw only the instrument panel and his immediate surroundings in the cockpit.

"I've been out cold," he announced. "Didn't the airscout turn turtle?"

He glanced around.

Yes. He knew it had turned over, but now it was right-side-up again.

"My gyroscopic restabilizer," he said proudly. "I forgot I'd invented it. It turned the airscout right-side-up after it crashed. It works!"

He peered out through the forward porthole directly over the instrument console, but saw nothing. It was too dark and murky outside.

"It's not night. What happened? Did I land in the trees?"

He got up and peered closer through the porthole. It was at that moment that he heard the gurgling.

"I must have lost some brake fluid," he muttered, turning and glancing down at the deck of the airscout. "Hmm, I don't remember that half inch of water on the deck."

Then he realized that the gurgling was a continuous sound now, rising steadily in pitch.

Startled, he stared at the porthole and reached up to

flick on the exodermal spotlight mounted on the prow of the airscout.

"As I feared," he said heavily, wiping the perspiration from his forehead. "Fish. Mammals. A string of algae. And some floating plankton. I'm in the water." He gave his beard a furious tug. "And sinking fast, too, if I'm not mistaken."

Zarkov stirred restlessly in the pilot seat. "Must have landed in one of those confounded swamps that dot the forest kingdom. Hit with a splash, but I was out cold. And by the looks of things, I'm sinking straight to the bottom!"

The gurgling rose in pitch and volume.

Zarkov felt his plyoboots suddenly fill with water as the incoming flood spilled over the tops. He lifted his feet and shook them.

"Never thought about landing in the water," he said thoughtfully. "Should have, though. Those early Earth astronauts always landed in the ocean. No way to get down gently in those days. Damn! I should have checked out those air-vent valves. I thought they were a-okay."

Zarkov moved the exodermal spotlight back and forth in the water. He saw the submarine life move upward as the airscout plummeted toward the bottom of the pond.

"Hmm. I could blow the oxygen capsule to equalize the air pressure against the water pressure, but I'd give myself the bends or worse." He shook his head. "Besides, I know I couldn't get enough oxygen into the airscout to equalize its weight and send it to the top."

Zarkov stroked his beard slowly.

The water was up to his waist now. And still the airscout sank further and further through the strange underwater world outside. Zarkov saw several starfish, and a deep-sea decapod with a quite lifelike face seemed to grin at him.

He shook his head musingly. He was getting hyperventilated because of the increase in air pressure in the airscout. The area in which the air was now compressed was equal to about half the interior of the airscout . . . Zarkov felt the pressure and the heat generated by the compression.

As he frowned thoughtfully, the airscout slammed to a stop and a great cloud of mud and slime rose before his eyes, obscuring the exodermal spotlight for a long moment.

The airscout sank a little further in the black muck and came to a teetering rest.

The spotlight penetrated the murk, which gradually settled. Zarkov saw that the mud came about to eye level.

"The damned thing is stuck and stuck good," he said matter-of-factly. "What do I do now?"

He reached into his pocket for a neuropill and swallowed it. He chewed thoughtfully.

"Bah! The damned things are supposed to calm you down. I'm not calm. I'm scared." He blew air out of his cheeks and fidgeted nervously in the seat. "You're a scientist, Zarkov, damn it! Why can't you think of something?"

The hatch? The hatch opened at the bottom and side of the airscout. If it opened at the dorsal, or top portion of the airscout, he could flip the dogs and escape with the bubble of air still inside the interior.

But with the hatch on the ventral surface, or bottom, he would have to blast out the carbon cartridges and take a chance on reaching the surface of the pond without any air bubble to protect him.

The water frothed up around his neck. He began to feel the intense pressure of both air and water against his body.

"I've got to do something—fast."

He fumbled with his flying gear and touched the backpack which contained his pop-out chute, his energy rations, and his spare blaster pistol. At least he had that! He slipped the blaster pistol into his waist belt and looked at the rations in the backpack. They were dry; the pack was wrapped securely in waterproof plyowrap.

Plyowrap! It was the most versatile of Mongo's all-purpose sheeting. Transparent, airtight, watertight, and unbreakable, it was self-sealing with a permanent bond when heated.

Zarkov unhitched the backpack and lifted it up above his head where the water had not yet reached. If he could remove the plyowrap outerskin from the pack, inflate it with the air left in the airscout, and seal the airpack around his head. . . .

Zarkov chuckled softly.

62

"I'd be a fool to call myself anything but a genius," he said, chortling. The water bobbed about his chin now, and still rose. "But I don't really have time to congratulate myself. Must get to work."

He quickly tore the plyowrap from the backpack, dropped the pack in the water, watched it emit bubbles as it cascaded to the deck, and quickly formed the plyowrap into a large balloonlike object, using a heat cube from the emergency pack commonly used for starting cooking fires.

He blew hard into the newly constructed balloon, feeling his temples throb with the exertion. The air inflated the plyowrap quickly, until it was pressing down into the water around Zarkov's ears. Soon the plyowrap balloon filled the entire space in the airscout where air had been.

Zarkov, underwater now, slowly enlarged the hole through which he had inflated the balloon, and slipped his head through it as if putting on a very tight ski cap. Now he had the balloon full of air around his head.

He picked up a wrench from the toolkit attached to the instrument console, and dove downward toward the hatch dogs. Quickly, he turned them from the inside, and the hatch loosened.

He pushed hard, sending the hatch out at a slanted angle. Oozing slime bulged over the top and poured up into the airscout. Zarkov quickly wriggled through the opening, his airbag balloon half-pulling him upward in the water.

As he pulled his boots through the opening, he realized the hatch was closing once again, and he had a moment's panic when his left boot caught in the steel jaws.

But after a fierce struggle, he was free and ascending quickly through the cloudy water.

The air in the balloon was very bad, and the pressure on him from the water made him dizzy. He kept spiraling upward, paddling his boots slightly, and making swimming motions with his hands.

Something slimy and scaly touched him on the side. He turned, looking out through the weird transparent balloon around his head. The water was lighter now, since he was obviously approaching the surface.

He saw an enormous tadpole, a good five feet in length, the first growth stage of Mongo's giant killer frogs.

It stared at him out of its slitted green eyes, and fish-tailed quickly away.

Zarkov broke surface a few seconds later, his body absolutely exhausted from immersion and pressure. He bobbed on the surface for a moment or two, the big balloon flailing in the air. Then, with an earth-quaking bang, it exploded.

The air which had been pressurized in the airbag escaped into the atmosphere.

Zarkov was stunned.

He sank.

The chill of the water revived him, and he swam for the surface again, blinking his eyes when he emerged into the air, trying to see where he was.

Enormous lily pads floated in the water, big enough for a dozen men to walk on. In the distance, he saw high oak trees with some type of hanging moss suspended from their branches. It was called mongomoss. Even though it was an unearthly bright yellow, it resembled Spanish moss.

Zarkov saw the shore, and he turned to make his way toward it.

He finally dragged himself up onto the bank and flopped down on his back. He wheezed and coughed.

He lay there, his eyes closed.

"I've had it," he said. "Just let me lie here."

Then he heard something.

One eye opened.

He stared.

Above him, not five feet away on the grassy bank of the swamp, stood a youth. He was dressed in a plain earth-colored tunic laced with leather thongs in the center. He had on roughspun trousers tucked into boots made of soft animal hide. He wore a skullcap with a bright-yellow feather, apparently from some alardactyl. Under the cap Zarkov saw long brown hair tied in a pirate's pigtail.

The youth stared down at him without a flicker of expression. In his hands he held a huge crossbow, longer than he was tall. He had it fully drawn. The arrow in the string was aimed directly at Zarkov's throat.

"Should ye move a muscle," said the youth in a voice which had not yet changed, "ye're a dead man."

"Friend," Zarkov said tiredly, trying to smile. "Friend,

64

do not mistake me for an enemy. I am a friend to those of the forest kingdon."

"Now, ye don't say so, do ye?" said the youth. "Ye nay would be pulling me leg?"

Zarkov sank back. He knew better than to try to argue, Forest-kingdom folk were a breed unto themselves. They were hard, being reared in adversity. They were stubborn by nature. And they were tough from necessity.

I can argue with any man on a scientific level, Zarkov thought. But when I argue with men on a lower level of intellect, I always lose.

He saw the gleam in the youth's brown eyes. He saw the arm tense and the string quiver.

Why am I not an orator or a politico? he wondered. Why am I not blessed with the golden tongue of the pol?

Zarkov could almost feel the metal tip of the arrow lodged in his throat.

CHAPTER 12

In his panic, Kial ran hard through the forest's undergrowth without further thought. He did not see the low-hanging branch and smashed headlong into it. The blow knocked him to the ground, where he lay for a moment before he came to his senses and sat up.

"Where am I going?" he asked himself. "What happened to Lari?" He shook his head and stood up, gazing fearfully about him.

He was in a deep part of the giant forest growth. He heard the sound of trees moving and branches snapping in the distance. It was the giant aphid coming after him. He knew that.

"Lari? I wonder what happened to Lari. I ran off. I never waited for him."

Kial moved through the woods and emerged in a small

clearing. There, across a draw, he saw the purple monster crouching in the trees, looking for him. A purple giant aphid.

Behind the beast, Kial saw the purple substance where Lari had been encapsulated by the aphid's spittle.

It's Lari! thought Kial. What happened to him?

Kial trembled.

"I should go to help Lari," he muttered. "But if I go, I may be killed by the beast. Perhaps Lari is already dead. How can I carry out the mission of Ming XIII if I, too, am dead?"

Kial nodded thoughtfully.

"I'll go into the woods and find the Tempendulum again. Then I can talk to Ming XIII and report the imprisonment of Lari."

He turned and moved through the thick trees. He had not gone more than a hundred yards before he stumbled over a metallic object in the underbrush. It had been covered over with branches to camouflage it.

Kial stared.

"The antimatter neutralizer ray gun!"

He and Lari had mounted it there on the ground when they had first come from the Tempendulum with it. It was at that spot that they had aimed it at Flash Gordon's jetcar and destroyed its suspension system.

"I can use it on the aphid!" Kial exclaimed, suddenly smiling in glee. "He can't get me!"

He turned to watch the aphid. It stood near the edge of the superway, looking over at Kial. Kial could not tell if it actually saw him or was simply searching for him. It did not matter. If he could set up the antimatter neutralizer, he could destroy the aphid.

Then he would be safe.

He pushed the branches away from the ray gun and cleared it out from the undergrowth. It came in two separate parts. There was a long slender barrel about six earth feet long, made of a dark-red translucent mineral that scientists had devised as the best medium for that type of laser destructor.

The laser rod in turn was mounted on a swivel gun base, with the base mounted on small wheels. The dials and solid-state mechanism of the ray gun were arrayed along a panel at the rear of the weapon.

Kial shifted the elevation and declination until he had the magniscope sights of the weapon centered on the large purple monster.

"Let's see," he said, puzzled. "Lari is the technician. I think I activate this lever." Kial flipped the lever.

He could hear an almost hushed whishing sound inside the laser rod.

Nothing happened.

Kial glanced at the dials and readout ports.

"Here it is. I've got it set at metal and hard minerals. I want to set it to animal flesh and soft-bone structure."

He turned the ray-intensity dial.

He heard the screech, and when he looked up to observe the aphid he saw that it was rapidly turning to a puff of cloudy vapor.

Then, as he watched, it quite suddenly was not there at all.

It was gone.

Kial flipped up the activator button.

The vapor of the destroyed giant insect vanished in the air above the mongospike growth in which it had stood.

Kial was stunned at the speed of the beast's destruction.

He walked through the brush, back to the spot where he had last seen Lari.

Poor Lari, he thought. If only he could have escaped.

But Lari was gone.

Again Kial shook his head sorrowfully.

As he stumbled down the slope of the draw, crossed the dried creekbed, and began to climb the opposite bank, he heard a sudden movement from the underbrush in front of him.

He froze.

Had the giant aphid rematerialized somewhere else?

He hid behind a thick overhang of moss. The noise moved toward him. It sounded almost like human footsteps.

He peered out to see what was coming.

Lari.

Kial was too shocked to speak.

Lari was brushing gobs of purple jelly off his clothes as

67

he walked along, looking repeatedly back over his shoulder. He seemed quite shocked.

Kial stepped out and stood in front of him.

Kial was bluffing. He had no idea how Lari had escaped from the blob of goo that had entrapped him.

"Hey," cried Lari, "How did you get the big monster?"

"The aphid?" said Kial with a superior snort. "It's gone. Vanished in a big cloud of smoke."

"I saw it. How did you do it?"

"I used the antimatter neutralizer ray gun!"

Lari nodded.

"How did you get away?"

Lari frowned. "That monster covered me with a lot of blob and I couldn't move. I saw you running away. Then after a little bit the monster seemed to come toward me. I thought he was getting ready to have me for dinner, but then there was a whirring sound and he disappeared."

"Right. I turned the neutralizer ray on him."

"Well, I was still frozen in that gunk. But after the monster vanished, suddenly the gunk melted. In fact, it did more than melt—it fell away and shriveled up into small pieces."

Kial rubbed his chin. "Probably the stuff has an affinity to the giant aphid. When the aphid was destroyed, then the gunk was destroyed, too."

"I guess so," agreed Lari.

"It's got to be that way."

"What do we do now, Kial?" Lari asked.

Kial considered. "Look. We know Flash Gordon and Dale Arden are dead. Now the only thing we have to do is to get rid of Prince Barin."

"Yeah," said Lari. "How do we do that?"

"Well, I think we'd better contact Ming XIII again."

"Right." Lari frowned. "How do we get to the Tempendulum?"

"I think it's in back of us. That way." Kial pointed past the spot where he had found the antimatter ray gun.

"Then let's go."

Kial stood still. "Hold it, dummy. I'm thinking."

"Well?"

"Ming XIII hasn't been very complimentary about our mission in the time probe."

"So?"

"Maybe we should take something back to him to prove we did get Gordon."

"That's a good idea," said Lari. "What?"

"Something like his military insignia. Or maybe his ring or his chronometer."

"Yeah. That makes sense."

Kial started through the underbrush to the top of the slope. Once there he could see across the area of mongo-spike almost to the superway. He stared in dismay.

"What's the matter?" Lari asked.

"Look!"

Lari came to the top of the rise and peered ahead. "It's Gordon. And that girl."

"They're alive."

CHAPTER 13

Astonished, Flash and Dale watched the tightly encompassing purple spittle with which the giant aphid had encapsulated them slowly turn a deeper color and then loosen its grip.

Immobile, they had watched through the purple jelly as Kial and Lari had startled the creature. They had seen Lari slowly enmeshed in the spittle and paralyzed in the same way they were. They had watched helplessly as Kial had fled into the forest.

And then they had seen the amazing destruction of the giant aphid as it had advanced into the forest. Before it had gone far, it had vanished in a cloud of smoke.

Then Kial had run toward them.

Moments later, the purple sputum in which they were so tightly enmeshed fell away from them. Then they could move their arms and legs, and walk. The purple matter clung to them in a kind of film.

69

"Are you all right?" Flash asked Dale.

"Y-y-yes," said Dale, trying to brush the jelly off her face and hair. "I think so."

"It was that disintegrator ray," said Flash. "The same thing that took out our suspension system. It simply dissolved the aphid."

"I suppose so," replied Dale, shaking her hair vigorously.

At that instant, Kial and Lari appeared at the edge of the superway with the two blaster pistols in their hands.

"All right, Gordon," said Kial. "I may have freed you from that monster, but you're not going anywhere."

"Who are you two, anyway?" Flash asked, walking toward them.

Dale followed.

"It's none of your business," Kial said threateningly.

"What do you want with us?" Flash persisted.

"Get back!" cried Kial, waving the blaster pistol.

Flash strode on, closing the distance between them.

"I'll zap you!"

Flash laughed. "Go ahead. Try. I recognize that pistol. It's mine. Try to zap me. I have a special safety device on that pistol to keep it from working for just anyone."

"You're lying," snapped Kial, but his face was contorted with doubt. He stared at the weapon.

"Kial!" cried Lari. "They're coming!"

"Right," said Flash, and he gave a sudden leap to the side as Kial aimed the blaster pistol at him. The blaster sizzled harmlessly, taking out the branches of a giant fern behind him.

"You lied to me," shouted Kial, twisting the blaster pistol to one side. "Stop!"

Flash ducked and launched himself in a low-flying tackle. His arms found Kial's legs and he quickly upended him. "It wasn't a lie," he said, chuckling. "It was a slight exaggeration."

They rolled together on the superway.

"I was a defensive back once." Flash laughed as he twisted Kial's neck. "I don't think you ever played the game, did you?"

Kial was gasping now and Flash's hands were around his throat. The blaster pistol had fallen to the surface of

70

the superway. Lari stood to one side, mouth open in shock.

"Flash!" cried Dale. "I can't reach the blaster pistol. You're rolling on it!"

"I don't know where you clowns got that blaster pistol of mine," Flash said grimly, "but it doesn't matter now. I'm glad I've got my hands on you, at last. I've been meaning to teach you a few manners."

Kial could say nothing. He was clawing at Flash's strong hands clamped around his throat.

Lari aimed his blaster pistol at Dale, but now he began to think about Kial. He saw that Flash had twisted Kial's arms around behind his back and was trussing him up with his belt.

"Hey!" cried Lari.

"Hey!" Flash responded.

Lari aimed the blaster pistol at Flash, but then saw that if he fired it he would disintegrate Kial, too.

Quickly, he shifted the pistol in his hand and slammed the handle at Flash's head.

Flash had turned when the hand grip of the pistol hit his skull.

He saw all the planets of Mongo's system, a couple of Earth suns, and the Milky Way.

Then nothing.

CHAPTER 14

Dale was scrambling onto the pavement toward the loose pistol dropped by Kial when Lari hit Flash and knocked him out. She had barely reached out for the weapon when she felt a blow on her own shoulder.

She fell.

Kial was up now, grinning at her, his mustache quivering. His boot lashed out and stepped on the blaster pistol.

The tips of Dale's fingers were pinched by the toe of Kial's boot.

"Ouch!" She drew back her hand.

Kial leaned over and grabbed the weapon. Dale tried to get to her feet, but she was off-balance.

She turned frantically. Flash lay on his side on the superway, holding his head in his hand, but unable to rise.

"You've stunned him!" cried Dale. "What is it you want with us?"

"We want Gordon," said Kial with an evil grin. He adjusted the blaster pistol in his hand and turned to study Flash as he lay at the edge of the roadway.

Dale leaped to her feet and grabbed Kial's arm. "No, you don't!" she cried.

Kial almost fell over. "Ah!" he said, leering. "You're one of those strong-willed women, are you? Lari, here's one that wants taming. Let's give her our lesson for the day, shall we?"

Lari was standing looking down at Flash Gordon. "You'd better do something about Gordon, Kial. I don't think he's going to like it when he finally comes to."

"Forget Gordon," Kial said, snorting. "We've got better prey now. Dale Arden, isn't it?" He turned to her.

"Yes, it's Dale Arden," snapped Dale. She faced Kial now, but she was afraid to make a move toward him. He had the blaster pistol trained on her.

"An earthling, like Gordon," said Kial.

"And proud of it," replied Dale. "Who are you? One of those Mingolites we're always having trouble with on Mongo?"

"It doesn't matter who we are," said Kial. "What matters is that we have you and Gordon and that's the reason we came here."

"You don't look like Mingolites," Dale said, puzzled. "Your clothes are weird. Another planet in Mongo's system?"

"Enough of this nonsense," said Kial. "Lari, come here. We're going to see if all the myths are true about Gordon and Dale Arden."

"Huh?" Lari asked.

"The myths say Gordon and his girl helped stabilize the country here for Prince Barin and his descendants. But

72

how can they with Gordon as good as dead and Dale Arden nothing but a puff of dust?"

"Kial!" shouted Lari.

Kial turned to him with annoyance.

Lari was pointing at Flash Gordon, who was shaking his head and trying to rise. He fell back.

"He'll never get up," snorted Kial.

"Get on with it," Dale interrupted. "If you're not going to use that blaster pistol, give it to me."

Kial grinned. "You'd like that, wouldn't you, lady?"

Dale stared him down.

"Now, now," said a voice that Dale knew very well, "didn't your mother ever tell you not to play with guns?" Flash? Dale glanced at the superway where Flash still lay, trying to make himself get up.

"Hey!" yelped Kial.

Dale wheeled around. Behind Kial, a tall figure with blond hair and blue eyes wrestled with Kial's right hand, which held the blaster pistol. Dale blinked. It was Flash Gordon! How—?

"What is this?" Kial cried, amazed.

Lari gaped. "It's Gordon!"

"Gordon?" repeated Kial, opening his hand to release the blaster pistol. "Gordon?"

Dale moved back away from Kial. She watched as Flash—for it was certainly Flash—wrestled with Kial and turned him around and around.

"It's just like dancing," Flash said merrily. "I'd rather have a more attractive partner, but if it has to be you then it has to be you."

"Shut up!" cried Kial.

"You shut up!" commanded Flash. He pulled quickly, twisted Kial's arm up in a hammerlock, and faced him, gripping him around the waist. "Now, get out of here and leave us in peace and quiet."

Kial was perspiring freely. He could not speak.

Flash spun him away and Kial fell into a heap on the superway.

Dale cried, "Look out, Flash! It's Lari!"

Flash turned quickly just as Lari ran at him, aiming the blaster pistol. Flash doubled up his fist and struck out at Lari's stomach.

73

"Ooof!" Lari said.

The blaster pistol spun through the air.

He went down on his back, staring at the sky.

Flash stood in the middle of the superway and dusted his hands. "Dale, are you all right?" he asked.

"Yes," said Dale. "But how did you do that?" She turned and pointed to the Flash on the superway, still lying there on his side.

"It's a long story," Flash began slowly.

Kial was crawling over the roadway away from Flash and Dale. "Lari, let's get out of here quick!"

"Yeah." Lari rolled over and got to his knees. "Right now!"

"Tell me," Dale said to Flash.

Flash grinned.

And, grinning, he vanished before her eyes.

Dale blinked.

"Flash!"

There was no answer.

She waved her hand out in front of her where she had touched Flash's chest a moment ago.

Nothing.

She turned and looked at Kial.

But he was gone.

And so was Lari.

All three were gone!

Dale did not know what to do.

"But they were all here a moment ago and now they're not here," she said nervously.

She turned to stare at Flash on the pavement.

He looked up at her, eyes blurred, but a game smile on his face.

"Wow!" he said. "That was some shot."

"Flash! How did you do that?"

"Do what, Dale?" Breathing heavily, Flash touched the back of his head where he had been hit by the butt of his own blaster pistol in Lari's hand.

"How did you knock them out?"

"No sale, Dale," Flash said, shaking his head. "I'm afraid I funked it. Didn't quite come off, you know, as Zarkov would say."

"You knocked them out and they disappeared!"

74

Flash glanced around. "They simply ran off; maybe you weren't watching carefully."

"They vanished. And so did you." Dale was close to tears of frustration.

"Me?" Flash touched his military uniform, his belt, his boots. "Vanished? I don't feel invisible."

Dale stormed at him. "Don't play with me, Flash. It isn't funny! How did you make yourself into a twin and get those two maniacs to leave?"

"I didn't," Flash said coolly. "Next question."

"If you don't tell me, I'll—I'll—"

"You'll scream," Flash said. "But it won't do you any good. You've imagined the whole thing." He frowned. "Although I certainly don't know why those two ran off the way they did."

"They didn't run off!" Dale shouted. "They vanished."

"The way I did," Flash murmured. He put his hand out and touched Dale's arm. "Come on, Dale. Let's get on our way to Arboria. I think the heat's gotten to you."

"The heat hasn't gotten to me and I'm just as sane as I ever was. What I want to know is how you made yourself appear in two places." Her face was red.

"I didn't do it," asserted Flash.

"I'll put my fist in your nose if you don't drop that male-superiority bit of yours."

"No, you won't," Flash said impishly, leaning toward her and grasping her wrist. "Calm down, and let's get on our way."

Dale bit her lip. "Oh, all right," she said in exasperation, pulling her arm away from Flash's grasp, "don't tell me."

"What's to tell?" Flash asked.

They began to walk along the superway.

Dale felt her good humor returning as they strode along. It was, as it had been, a beautiful day, with the sky showing clear above the trees and the forest sounds returning to normal about them.

A silvery monkey flashed through the branches, leering down at them. An alardactyl of a luminescent orange plumage chased after some creature in the brush. The flyworts bleeped in the distance.

"We should be close to Arboria, don't you think?" Dale asked.

Flash smiled. "Yes, I do think. I'm glad to see you're back to normal after your, er, aberration."

Dale shook her head. "You're not going to make me get mad at you, no matter how hard you try. I swear there were two of you and one of you disappeared."

"Nothing disappears, really. It's an illusion."

"That blaster pistol of yours vanished!"

Flash frowned. "I think I must have simply misplaced it."

"But those two hoodlums had it. And they had mine as well."

Flash nodded. "That's something we've got to find out about when we get to Arboria."

Dale nodded. "All right, but it's like witchcraft. Two men disappear one time. Our zarcar is ruined. Two men return and vanish again. You appear and disappear." She shook her head. "Too much seems to be happening all at once."

"There's some logical explanation for it," Flash said insistently.

They rounded a turn in the superway and Flash pointed with a triumphant gesture.

"There it is. Arboria!"

In truth, it was Arboria. They both saw it through the slant of the roadway and the arch of the trees. It was exactly the same as they had remembered it: an entire city, molded out of giant trees and branches. The city itself rested on a foundation of giant live timber that had been formed into apartments and rooms and chambers of all kinds. The upper city had then been fashioned from wood on top of the trees, with great vistas and parks and streets made out of reconstituted wood fibers called celluloplast.

They should be there in minutes.

Flash took Dale's arm and walked faster.

Dale smiled.

She looked again at the city, always fascinated by its naturalness, its forestry feel, its singular haunting woodsy beauty and—

There was no city there.

Arboria had vanished.

Like Kial. Like Lari. Like Flash.

Vanished.

Flash halted in his tracks. "It's gone!" he gasped.

"There's got to be some logical explanation," Dale replied mockingly.

"But—but—"

Flash got down on his hands and knees, feeling the pavement of the superway.

"What are you doing?"

He crawled along the surface.

Dale was frightened. "Have you gone mad?"

"The superway!" Flash whispered. "It's different."

"Different?"

"A moment ago it turned to the right, Dale," said Flash. "Now it goes straight, upward, and then to the left!"

Dale stared.

She closed her eyes. She could still see the superway in her memory.

Flash was right.

She opened her eyes and put her hand to her mouth. Her hand trembled.

"Flash, I'm frightened."

Flash stood, gripping her hand.

"There's some—"

"I know. There's a logical explanation for all this!" Dale intoned sardonically.

Flash turned and stared blankly at her.

"What is it?"

CHAPTER 15

The youth who held the poised crossbow on Zarkov moved back a fraction of an inch. For a moment, a flicker of doubt showed in his eyes.

"Where do ye hail from, outlander?"

The arrow was still aimed at Zarkov's throat.

"If we're to talk," Zarkov said, "I think you'd better aim that crossbow somewhere else, if you please. It makes me nervous. You wouldn't want to impede my free flow of speech, would you?"

A faint smile crossed the youth's face. Zarkov could see that the boy was extremely handsome, without yet even the down of a beard on his face.

"Ye have a sense of humor, outlander," the youth said admiringly.

"And a sense of proportion," Zarkov added quickly. "As I trust you have, too. Now, if you'll kindly put that bow aside."

"Ye swam the dismal swamp?" asked the youth, his eyes flicking across the giant lily pads and the fluorescent islands of algae on the surface of the morass.

"Dismal swamp," repeated Zarkov with a smile. "Aptly named. I swam it, youth."

"Sar," amended the youth, his eyes narrowing.

"Sar?" Zarkov laughed. "Perhaps we're related. I'm Zar. Zarkov."

The brown eyes jumped. "A strange name for one of Arboria. By yer dress I assume ye to be of Barin's kingdom."

"Yes," said Zarkov. "And you?"

The crossbow relaxed. "I am a simple country boy," Sar said with satisfaction. With a deft movement, he slipped the arrow into the quiver looped around his shoulder. "The forest is home to me."

"Excellent. I have come on a mission from Prince Barin."

Sar moved over to Zarkov. "And the swamp?"

"My airscout crash-landed. I was unwary enough to select the dismal swamp as a landing place." Zarkov smiled wryly.

"By the manner of yer speech, I do not think ye be a native of Arboria."

Zarkov shook his head. "I am from a planet called Earth in a distant solar system."

The youth nodded. "And for what reason would ye be flying an airscout across the forest kingdom?"

"Two friends are lost along the superway from the spaceport to Arboria."

"It is merely a matter of twenty miles," reflected the youth. "How could it be that they have lost their way?"

"The question had occurred to us," said Zarkov. "That is why I set out in the airscout."

"And who do ye refer to as 'us'?"

"Prince Barin and I."

"Ye are acquainted personally with Prince Barin?" the youth asked in surprise. "It is a privilege. The brave Prince Barin and his wife, Veta."

Zarkov's eyes were very still. "Veta? That is not the Princess Barin I know, Sar."

Sar smiled flatly. "I am merely practicing caution, Zarkov. And the Princess's name is actually—?"

"Aura, if it is any business of yours. The daughter of Emperor Ming."

Sar sighed. "Then you really are Dr. Zarkov."

Zarkov was amused. "You have heard of me?"

"Everyone knows of Dr. Zarkov. Sire, I am not quite such a simple country boy as I may seem to be. I am an agent of Prince Barin's intelligence council. The I.C., as it is called."

"A very secret group," Zarkov replied quietly. "I have heard of it."

"Then you know that we patrol the entire forest kingdom, searching out infiltrators from Mingo and other enemies of the state."

Zarkov laughed. "Your accent is slipping."

Sar nodded. "I know you, Zarkov. I respect you, but I had to be sure you were not an agent in disguise from Ming's realm."

"No, I'm the real thing."

"I believe you. Now, how can I serve you?"

"By helping me find the superway. I must find my friends."

"Who are they?" Sar asked.

"Flash Gordon and Dale Arden."

"They are in the forest kingdom?" Sar asked, surprised.

"Yes. They returned last night from Earth. There is a celebration scheduled for this afternoon in Arboria. We are honoring Prince Barin for the liberation of Mongo from the despotism of Ming the Merciless."

"I know all about that," said Sar. "That is the reason I am near the border of Mingo." He hesitated.

"You have a special reason for being here?" Zarkov asked.

"Not really," the youth said cautiously. He avoided Zarkov's eyes. "Come," he said, "let's get started for the superway. It's only a mile or two through the woods."

"Good," said Zarkov. "I would never have found it by myself."

Sar smiled. "That's right."

"You don't have to agree with me so readily," grumbled Zarkov.

The forest was thick, giant conifers sending branches and needles high into the air. Their thick trunks crowded one another, leaving barely enough room to pass. The path led over a thick mat of cones and needles that had lain there for centuries. An undergrowth of bear's-paw ferns with huge fronds presented a stiff resistance, against which they struggled continually for passage.

Flying mammals and leaping tree lizards shot through the foliage all around them. Red-and-orange tree rodents flashed briefly in the dapples of sunlight. A giant alardactyl screeched high in the air.

Then all was silence.

It was a cathedral-like silence that Zarkov remembered from Earth and the days he had spent in church as a boy.

Only the sound of their own boots crunching through the coniferous residue on the forest floor could be heard.

"Oof!" Sar cried.

Zarkov whirled around to see what the trouble was.

He never found out.

A heavy weight smashed against him from above and bore him to the ground, where he twisted and turned, trying to get away from some active force that held him firmly in its grasp.

He saw the scarlet cloak then, and the body of a large fellow who jumped out of a tree and was now aiming a huge rocklike fist at his chin.

Zarkov struggled to reach his blaster pistol. He saw the face of his assailant. The man's complexion was an amaz-

80

ing indigo blue, which made his yellow eyes even more re-markable.

As he flailed about, Zarkov saw Sar struggling with an-other ruffian in a crimson cloak. That man, too, was blue. Sar was not doing too well; he could not seem to fight very well. His crossbow lay broken in two on the ground.

That made Zarkov renew his own efforts against the man who had jumped him. At least, he thought, there were only two ambushers, not more.

"Here, here!" bellowed Zarkov. "Why are you attacking us? We're honest fellows, much like yourselves."

"Forest-kingdom rabble," the blue man growled. "Rab-ble."

Zarkov had his blaster pistol loose now. He aimed it at his assailant's stomach. But suddenly, he found himself flat on his back in the needles looking up into the man's slightly tilted yellow eyes.

Zarkov's blaster pistol was gone, kicked away by the blue man's booted foot.

The blue man was dressed in a stretchsuit beneath the crimson cloak. The stretchsuit was made of an iridescent type of plyoweave, which caught dots of sunlight, making the surface dance. It was a garment much like an old-fashioned leotard and was colored in an ink-blot design of orange on yellow. Inside the crimson cloak, the effect was one of some kind of exotic grasshopper. The man wore a skullcap of red to cover an obviously bald blue head.

"Cease!" he commanded, his voice deep and firm, but tinged with a very heavy Mingolite accent. From his plyoweave stretchsuit he drew a curved dagger of duro-plast and placed the sharp edge of his boot on Zarkov's throat. "One move, and I'll separate your gizzard from your backbone!"

Zarkov shrugged.

"Captain Slan," said the other blue man, who was dressed in an identical costume. "I have the forest youth secured. And his ancient weapon is inoperative."

Captain Slan smiled faintly. He stared at Zarkov. "And I have the old man in hand."

"Old man!" Zarkov boomed. "Listen, you yellow-livered poachers, you'd better have a good explanation for this in-decency."

81

Slan laughed loudly. "Lieutenant Brod, let's teach these two a lesson, shall we?"

Brod was already securing Sar's hands behind his back as Slan prodded Zarkov to his feet and twisted a pliable metallic cord around Zarkov's wrists.

Zarkov looked at Sar and gave him a reassuring wink. Sar's eyes mirrored his fright. He looked at Zarkov with concern.

Lieutenant Brod pushed Sar against the enormous bulk of a tree trunk and shoved him hard into the bark with a blow to the chest. Sar cried out in pain. Brod's blue face looked startled. His little yellow eyes glittered.

He reached out and as Zarkov watched in horror he tore the cap from Sar's head and dashed it and the yellow feather to the ground. Sar's hair was long and brown and soft.

Quickly Brod reached out and ripped the tunic apart. Underneath the tunic Sar wore a thin body stocking of plyoweave.

Brod grinned and uttered a leering chuckle.

Under the loose tunic, Sar was utterly feminine in shape.

"A girl!" Zarkov cried in surprise.

Captain Slan's eyes gleamed as he surveyed the face and body.

"A beautiful catch for the emperor's harem," he gurgled in delight. "Perhaps the emperor will excuse us if she arrives in a slightly used condition."

Lieutenant Brod roared his approval.

Captain Slan shoved Zarkov against the tree trunk and moved over to Sar. He reached out and ripped the tunic from her shoulders.

Then he grabbed the thin sheath of plyoweave at the throat.

CHAPTER 16

Underneath the protection of a giant maidenhair fern, Kial and Lari faced each other. Kial was angry, Lari frightened.

"What are we going to do?" Lari asked in a trembling voice.

"How do I know what we're going to do?" asked Kial. "You bungled the whole thing!"

"Bungled?" Lari yelped, very hurt. "That second Flash Gordon came out of nowhere."

"You had the drop on him," Kial said accusingly. "You could have zapped him."

"I don't know what you're talking about."

"You didn't zap him. You let him get to us and disarm us."

"I didn't let him disarm us. I was trying to hit him, then he had me. You had the blaster pistol. Why didn't you use it?"

"Because, dummy, you were in the way. I couldn't kill him without killing you." Kial stroked his chin thoughtfully. "Come to think of it, I suppose that would have been the best thing to do."

Lari pouted. "Come on, Kial. Think of something. We can't report back to Ming XIII and tell him what happened."

Kial shook. "Absolutely not! Let's think hard, Lari. Let's put our minds to it and—"

"I've got it!" exclaimed Lari. "Let's give Flash and Dale the time belts and send them five centuries back in time."

"Dummy, they'd be as mobile as we are now. And we'd be stuck here."

"I'd rather be stuck here than go back to the future and Ming XIII."

Kial nodded. "Of course, there's that point."

"How about this? We move the neutralizer ray ahead of the two of them, on the road to Arboria, and zap them as they pass."

There was a pause. "No," replied Kial, after deep thought.

"Why not?"

"Because they'd see us from Arboria. Flash and Dale are just about to Arboria right now. Probably in sight of it on the superway."

"So?"

"They've got guards on the city walls. They'd see us and that would ruin everything. Then the palace would be alerted to trouble and Prince Barin would go underground."

"What's Prince Barin got to do with it?"

Kial snapped his fingers. "Wake up, dummy. That's the mission Orto and Lanl are assigned to."

"What mission?"

"The assassination of Prince Barin."

"I didn't know that," replied Lari, wide-eyed.

"You just don't listen, dummy."

"If only we could move the city, we could ambush them and not be seen from the city."

Kial blinked. "What did you say?"

"I said, if only we could move the city. . . ."

"How could we move the city?" Kial stared. "Wait a minute! If we can go back into time far enough, before the city was built, we could change the plans and move the city's location. That's what you mean, isn't it?"

"It is?" Lari asked blankly.

Kial's eyes narrowed. "No good. That's too tough. Look. It's the roadway—that's the key. If we go back in time and move the roadway, make it wind around instead of going straight to Arboria, then we've gained a couple miles of walking space. We sit in the woods, we kill Flash and Dale while they're walking toward Arboria, nobody sees us, and we're home-free."

"That's right," said Lari.

"You're smarter than I thought you were, Lari," said Kial sarcastically.

"Yeah. What was that with the stakes, Kial?"

"Shut up, dummy! Let's get moving. The computer readout on that superway showed it was built twenty years before Flash and Dale used it. We set our time belts to that date, to minus three two one wye, and we move the stakes."

"What year, Kial?"

"Three oh one and twenty is three twenty-one. Three two one. Just follow orders, dummy. You'll make out with me running things."

"Yeah."

They were off by seven months and four days, but by moving back and forth in time they finally found the correct day and stood on the projected roadway from the spaceport to Arboria. A line of surveyor's stakes enclosed the borders of the wide superway.

"Flash and Dale are just about there," said Kial, pointing. "So we simply break the road off here, move it around in a big sweeping circle, and change the stakes so it'll be built in a wide arc instead of straight. Got it?"

"Sure, Kial," replied Lari blankly.

"Then come on, let's get at it!"

They pulled up the stakes and carried them through the woods. It was a hard job. They extended the road at least an extra two miles. By moving the stakes and by cutting and stripping fifty more from the woods, they managed to extend the roadway so Arboria could not be seen from the far arc of the wide curve.

It was hard, exhausting work.

"They'll be in Arboria by now," wailed Lari.

"Dummy, we're in the past now! We can go back to the exact instant they both saw Arboria. What's the matter with you? We're working back twenty years before."

"I guess I don't understand," said Lari despondently.

"Just shut up and pound."

Finally, after four hours, Kial and Lari stood by the side of the projected roadway and Kial gazed in satisfaction at their work.

"Good. We'll travel forward in time now and be ready for them."

"Yeah," said Lari.

"Set your time belt," Kial commanded. He fiddled with

the digital readout on his own.

Instantly they stood beside the superway, already built, curving around a carefully cambered bend in the dense forest out of sight of Arboria.

Kial looked gleeful. "We did it! We did it!"

Lari looked around. "Where's the antimatter neutralizer?"

"Yeah," said Kial. "I've got to go look for it. You stay here, dummy. I've got to get a fix on the location of the gun."

Lari sat down.

Kial looked into the forest and started down the superway. "I think it's over there somewhere."

He found it without a great deal of trouble, returned, and brought Lari back with him to lug the parts to the side of the superway where they would wait.

Finally, when they had the neutralizer gun set up, Kial turned the laser rod barrel in the direction of the superway.

Lari peered through the magniscope sights. "That should hit them when they come in sight, Kial," he said. "You're a genius."

"I know," said Kial. He grinned. "Now we just sit here and we wait. It shouldn't be long."

"Right," said Lari.

They sat down under the shade of a giant horsetail plant. It was an evergreen rushlike herb with yellow-jointed stems and without leaves or flowers.

Kial drew out a packet of bananacco and started to roll a smoke. As he lit the highstik with a heat cube, he handed Lari the sack and watched him roll his own.

Soon they were both puffing and watching the superway.

"There they are," Lari said in a shaky voice.

Kial nodded, stubbed out his highstik and moved quickly to the sights of the neutralizer gun. He crouched behind it and flicked the magniscope into operation. He could see the two Earthlings clearly.

"I've got them zeroed in," he told Lari.

"Then zap them and let's get back home."

Kial shook his head. "I can't say I trust this equipment all that much. You know how our scientists are. Remember we missed that location when we set our flying belts for the site by the Tependulum? I don't want to miss again. I'll let them get a little closer."

Lari shrugged. He puffed on his highstik and watched the little clouds of smoke roll toward the seventh sun of Mongo.

Finally Kial said, "I'm ready, Lari. You want to double-check me?"

Lari came to the ray gun and peered through the magniscopic sights. "You're on target," he said, puffing away.

Kial got behind the sights and reached out for the laser button.

"Good-bye, Flash! Good-bye, Dale!" he said, and laughed as he pushed in the activator.

CHAPTER 17

The superway wound through a thick stand of giant conifers. Ahead Flash and Dale saw only more roadway. There was no sign of any jetcars along the pavement, nor was there any sign of Arboria in the distance.

"It's dark here," said Dale. "I never knew the forest was so thick."

Flash nodded. "This is one of the most primitive sections of it, Dale. These trees are over ten thousand years old."

"It's creepy," Dale said, shuddering.

"You're still imagining things." Flash smiled.

"I didn't imagine seeing Arboria. You saw it, too."

"That's right. At least, I thought I saw it." He looked at Dale. "Just the way you thought you saw a second me back there when those two ruffians tried to kill us."

"I didn't imagine that; I saw you." Dale held her chin up stubbornly.

"Well, maybe it's mass hypnosis. I mean, the second

Flash Gordon. And the glimpse of Arboria before it vanished."

"And the roadway changing like that," Dale added.

Flash rubbed his chin thoughtfully. "I haven't figured that one out yet."

"I know. But you're sure there's a logical explanation for it," Dale said sarcastically.

"Right."

Dale shook her head. "You're impossible."

They trudged on in silence. Silver monkeys played in the trees, then disappeared. They could be heard chattering in the foliage.

"Flash, I think—" Dale halted beside him in the road.

Flash turned. "What, Dale?"

Dale stared into the darkened woods ahead. "I think I see something in there."

"Monkeys?" Flash laughed.

"No, I think it's a man."

"In the trees?" Flash asked, frowning and looking into the dense foliage. "I don't see anything."

Dale stamped her foot. "Oh, you think I'm going crazy, but I'm not!"

Flash smiled. "I don't think you're going crazy. Some very strange things have been happening to us today."

"Do you think—?" Dale began. "I mean, those two men. Could they be there ahead of us—waiting?"

"They could be," Flash said quietly. "Anyone who can disappear the way those two did could be anywhere."

"Let's turn back," Dale suggested abruptly.

"We can't," said Flash gently. "We've got to get on to Arboria. Zarkov and Prince Barin will wonder what's happened to us."

Dale sighed. "Oh, all right. It's so far. Really, I never thought I'd be so tired."

They walked a few more steps in silence.

"It does seem a long way to the city," said Flash. "Wait a minute, up ahead—see? It's a road marker. We can verify how far we've got to go to the city."

"Good," said Dale. "My feet are tired."

They walked over to the side of the superway, where the large stone had been set up beside the pavement.

"It says four Earth miles," Flash observed with some concern. He looked at Dale.

"But we just passed a marker that said two Earth miles, just before we saw the city the first time!" Dale cried.

"I know," agreed Flash softly. "Something very strange is happening." He had walked around the marker and was staring down at the other side. "Dale!"

She joined him. "What is it?"

He pointed. "Would you look at that?"

On the far side of the stone someone had scrawled in pencil:

FLASH AND DALE—THE ANSWER IS THIS WAY.

After the words, an arrow had been drawn, pointing into the woods at their deepest part.

Flash gazed into the dense foliage where the conifers were so tightly spaced that there was barely room to pass.

"What shall we do?" Dale asked softly.

"Is someone trying to play an elaborate joke on us?" Flash wondered.

"No one would joke with us," said Dale. Her eyes lighted up. "Except Dr. Zarkov!"

"But this doesn't seem like a Zarkov jest. This seems—" Flash stopped after a moment and stood, thinking.

"Seems what?" Dale prompted him.

"I don't really know," Flash admitted ruefully.

Dale stared at the writing. "Look," she said impulsively. "I know who wrote that."

Flash frowned. "Who?"

Dale looked into Flash's eyes. "You."

"Come on, now!" snorted Flash.

"But it's your handwriting. I could tell it anywhere."

Flash peered more closely. It did look like his handwriting, at that. Especially the fancy flourish on the capital F at the beginning of his name. It was his writing. But how?

"How could I have written it?" he scoffed. "You were with me. How could I have gotten ahead of you in the road?"

"I don't know." Dale considered. "Maybe you did it a long time ago. Last year, maybe."

"Don't be silly," said Flash. He glanced around. "Look, I think we'd better take a chance. Do you want to?"

"Follow the arrow?" Dale asked.

"Yes."

She nodded. "I was going to suggest that, anyway."

Flash said, "It points right into the thickest part of the woods. Are you game?"

"Sure."

"Let's go."

They stumbled at first, going through the rocks and clods next to the superway, but finally the footing improved. By that time they were walking through thick forest, their path a winding needle-covered way between the towering trees.

It was suddenly very quiet.

Dale took hold of Flash's arm. "I'm scared."

"If we don't find anything in a minute, we'll go back," Flash assured her.

The woods ended abruptly.

They stood at the edge of the forest, looking across a small clearing surrounded by enormous conifers.

In the center of the clearing, there was a large structure built in the shape of a hemisphere.

It was the Tempendulum, although they did not know it by that name.

Flash stared. "What is it?"

Dale shook her head. "It looks like some kind of green-house. You know, where they grow plants."

Flash patted her hand. "I'm going over to it."

"Be careful," Dale said.

"You stay here. If anything happens to me, get out of here quick."

"All right." Dale felt herself trembling.

Flash strode out into the open, glancing up at the big yellow sun of Mongo. It was Mongo's seventh sun, in many ways the longest-lived and the best. The other six suns had burned out millions of years ago, according to Mongo's history.

There wasn't a cloud in the sky and the heat of the sun felt good on Flash's back.

He glanced quickly around as he proceeded through the low brush. It resembled chaparrall back on Earth. The growth was mixed in with wild mongospike. As he neared the gleaming metallic hemisphere, Flash found a small porthole in one of the segments of the structure.

Inside he could see a spacious emptiness that seemed laced with flickering vibrations of light.

He looked back at Dale. She stood, watching him with fear in her eyes.

Flash walked up to the hemispheroid and reached out to touch it. It was warm metal, heated by the rays of the sun.

Nothing happened.

He climbed the steps and peered in through the port-hole of the big dome.

He saw an instrument console at one end of the entry-way, and a long pendulum that hung down from the apex of the dome. Several astro-seats, resembling those used by astronauts in weightless environmental rockets, were spaced out near the pendulum. Loose straps dangled from their arms.

In the middle of the dome, a globe with a slightly oblate shape floated in the air. It was opaque, jet black, and it seemed sharply alive somehow.

Flash turned and waved to Dale.

"Come on. It's some kind of experimental laboratory."

Dale hurried breathlessly through the underbrush.

"Maybe it is Dr. Zarkov's toy. Maybe he was playing some elaborate joke on us."

Flash jumped down onto the floor of the dome. As he did so, he knelt and tentatively touched the surface with his palm.

"What's the matter?" Dale asked.

Flash stood, his eyes clouded. "Dale, look at the metal. What is it?"

"Oh, some kind of rolled sheet steel, perhaps?"

Flash shook his head. He looked at Dale, puzzled. "It's nothing like that. I don't even recognize the element it's made of, Dale!"

"What are you trying to say?"

Flash had wandered over to the console where the digital readouts were assembled on a wide board.

"And look at these instruments," he said, pointing to the console.

Dale studied them. "What are they?"

"I have no idea," said Flash. "The readout numbers are familiar. But the initials don't make sense. T.C. V.E. E.T.Z." Flash shook his head. "It makes no sense to me. The dome is immobile. It's not going anywhere. Then why the travel instruments?"

Dale leaned over and studied the face of a dial where a golden needle wavered over a series of strange cabalistic signs.

"What language is that?" she asked hopelessly.

Flash shook his head. "It's not English, and it's not Mongo, or any of its variants. That's for sure."

Dale turned and stared at the large opaque black globe that floated in the center of the dome.

"Flash! Look at that globe, would you? It's almost as if it contained thousands and thousands of watts of pure light and energy. You can see how it almost shines through the black opaque shell."

Flash blinked. "It's almost like an adaptation of the old light box—the camera obscura—but it doesn't let in light, it holds in light!"

"Why?"

"I don't know." He smiled faintly. "Wish we had Zarkov here. He'd tell us."

"Or make a good stab at it," said Dale.

The black opaque globe suddenly trembled in the air, where it hung suspended as if by levitation. Then it sizzled, as if the light inside were performing some delicately assigned task.

Simultaneously there was a sound in the woods outside the dome.

Flash rushed to the porthole of the strange hemispheroid.

Someone stood just inside the darkness of the forest surrounding the clearing.

Then, quite quickly, whoever it was vanished into thin air.

The floating light trap sizzled and moved toward the large pendulum that hung from the apex of the dome.

The pendulum glowed and gave off a brief but staggering amount of heat.

Dale fell back, stunned.

Flash grabbed at her.

And the strange metallic floor under their feet moved.

CHAPTER 18

With his hands hidden between his back and the trunk of the tree, Zarkov twisted and turned until he had wrested one hand free. The pliable cord dropped to the ground. Zarkov eyeballed the needle-covered earth near the trunk of the tree until he found the gleam of his blaster pistol lying in a tangle of pine cones and pebbles.

Captain Slan's attention was focused on Sar as he tore the plyoweave stretchsuit away from her throat. Lieutenant Brod's eyes gleamed and his mouth hung open in lugubrious anticipation. Sar twisted her head back and saw Zarkov move from the tree trunk. Instantly, she understood what he was doing.

She screamed loudly, flailing her arms to make sure neither Slan nor Brod saw Zarkov. Slan drew back, cursing. Brod grabbed for the girl's arms and pushed her against the tree.

"Hold her there," Captain Slan snarled. "She's a hellcat for sure." His blue face glistened with perspiration. "But a pretty one, at that."

Lieutenant Brod giggled and thrust Sar hard against the tree trunk while Slan lifted his hand once again to demolish her plyoweave stretchblouse. Sar screamed dutifully.

Zarkov held the blaster pistol in his right hand, moving around to the side where he had a perfect angle of fire on Captain Slan.

"Get away from her, Slan, if that's your name!" Zarkov boomed commandingly.

Slan whirled, his face frozen, his yellow eyes wide and startled in his indigo face. His mouth opened in surprise, revealing bright-yellow teeth the same color as his eyes. The molars were pointed, the canines twice as long as the molars.

"Up on top of your head with your hands—both of you," Zarkov ordered.

Slowly they complied.

"Brod, you fool," muttered Slan, watching Zarkov with his big cat's eyes. "You've done it again."

Brod gurgled in his throat. "Captain Slan," he whined. "I swear to you, he was thoroughly secured when I left him."

"You, too, Brod," bellowed Zarkov, waving the blaster pistol at him. "Get away from her and stand out over there." He indicated a clear place in the wooded terrain. "Hands up!" he snapped as Slan began to ease his hands downward from his head.

"You're making a mistake," snapped Slan as he moved away from the tree trunk where Sar now leaned in exhaustion and relief. "We've got you surrounded here."

Out of the corner of his eye, Zarkov saw Brod make a sudden movement toward his own back. Instantly Zarkov whirled and fired the blaster pistol. Brod stiffened and toppled over backward on the forest turf.

Slan's yellow eyes narrowed. They seemed to be burning in his head. His tongue flicked out briefly and licked his upper lip. The tongue was almost as yellow as the teeth, Zarkov noticed in disgust. Slan smiled and nodded agreeably at Zarkov.

"It's an amazingly precise weapon," he said in the same gurgling voice Brod had used. "How is it energized?"

Zarkov smiled. "It's a complicated mechanism, blue man, and quite probably well beyond your limited intelligence to comprehend."

"Of course," Slan said with a wide grin. Zarkov was unable to look at the yellow teeth and the flick of the yellow tongue. "Of course, but one always loves to learn. Tell me, is it one of Prince Barin's mechanisms?"

"Earth," said Zarkov negligently.

"Ah. That other solar system not far from ours." He smiled gently. He moved imperceptibly nearer Zarkov, his hands still over his head where the bright red skullcap was affixed to his blue bones. "You Earth people have brought

94

great treasures of commerce and science to the backwoods people of the forest kingdom," he said purringly.

He looked, for all the world, like a large blue cat, Zarkov thought suddenly. He laughed. "Indeed we have. And they're all the better for it, I can tell you that."

"Yes," Slan whispered, nodding.

Zarkov's eyes were riveted to Slan's yellow ones. He felt as if he did not want to move ever again. Suddenly, he heard Sar's frightened scream.

"Look out, Zarkov! He's hypnotizing you. He's going to take your weapon."

Zarkov could feel himself growing nerveless, and with the last vestiges of his willpower, he squeezed on the hand grip of the blaster pistol. The great blue body stiffened under the sizzling impact of the weapon's force and then keeled over backward, the yellow eyes rolling up into the blue head. With a crash, the body hit the pine needles.

Sar ran over to Zarkov, looking up at him with her big brown eyes.

"Thanks, Sar," Zarkov said loudly. "I guess he was playing me for a sucker, wasn't he?"

"Yes," said Sar, leaning down over the blue body. "But you got him before he could put you under."

"Must be some kind of hypnosis, as you said," Zarkov responded, stroking his wiry beard with a frown. "Those yellow eyes." He shuddered. "They're enough to do anyone in."

Sar shook her head. "I don't recognize this breed. Blue men. We haven't run across that combination in the chromosome charts of Mongo. Must be some mutant from the unexplored portions of the planet. The Boiling Desert. Or the Ultimate Icepack."

Zarkov knelt beside Sar. He touched the blue skin. "Flesh and bone structure exactly like ours. But that blue color! And those yellow eyes and teeth!" Zarkov shuddered. "And did you see that tongue?"

Sar swallowed hard. "There's a reptilian scaliness to the man's flesh. Do you note that? Perhaps it's a throwback to an earlier era."

"Could be," murmured Zarkov. "No one would breed selectively for those characteristics, would they?"

Sar stood up. "I've got to report in to Prince Barin.

95

This is very important news. You heard what he said—that we are surrounded."

"May be a bluff," Zarkov growled, standing beside her. "It could just be a clever ploy to scare us."

Sar turned to Zarkov. "I'm sorry I had to play games with you, Dr. Zarkov. My name isn't Sar. It's Sari. And I've found it much better to stake out in the forest kingdom as a man than as a wench." She smiled faintly. "It's much less tempting to the vagrants and outlaws in the woods around here. Forgive me?"

Zarkov boomed out a loud laugh. "Forgiven."

"Also, I was out here to gather specific information. We've known for a long time that some new contingent of undesirables was invading the border areas. Because we didn't know the leader's name, we couldn't decide exactly which division of Ming's army was being utilized. This looks like an entirely new operation—a new mutant breed of fighters out of Ming's laboratories."

Zarkov shivered. "They certainly scare me."

"I've got to get back as soon as I can and report in to Minister Hamf."

Zarkov pondered. "Shall we split up? Or go on together?"

"Together," Sari said decisively. "There's an inn near the pine forest. I'll call into Arboria on the laserphone there."

"If you're sure I won't hinder you," Zarkov said with a toothy smile.

"Not at all." Sari studied the blaster pistol which Zarkov still held in his hand. "That's a beautiful weapon."

Zarkov nodded. "I've added a few nuances of my own to it," he said in satisfaction. "But it's a standard Earth neutralizer. Nitrogen-operated. Standard feedback mechanism. I've made my own variable controls. Freezes. Stuns. Impedes. Smashes. Repels. Flattens. Kills. Immolates. Hydrogenates. Aerates. Obliterates."

"All with that one weapon?"

"It's just something I've added to the standard specs. Here, I'll show you." Zarkov held out the blaster pistol to Sari. "You see it's on KILL now." Zarkov blinked, and shook the weapon hard. "Damn! Now it isn't on KILL at all. I had it on STUN, the next-to-least powerful position."

96

Zarkov turned to stare at Slan. "We can't have that! I thought I'd killed him! Stun? He'll come to in a half hour."

"Just reset the blaster and finish the job."

Zarkov nodded grimly. "Of course." He struggled with the force-adjuster lever on the side of the weapon.

"Well?" Sari asked.

"The damned thing is jammed," Zarkov bellowed, banging the blaster pistol against the trunk of the nearest tree. "Would you look at that? It's on STUN! I can't get it to move to KILL!"

Sari glanced at the two unconscious blue men. "Let's get out of here, Dr. Zarkov. If they're going to come to, we would be wise to get out of the vicinity."

"I won't leave until I get this weapon fixed," Zarkov muttered darkly. "It must have been damaged when Brod kicked it out of my hand."

Sari looked around at the woods. "Quickly, Dr. Zarkov. We'll have to take our chances with them. I want to be far away when they revive."

Zarkov threw the blaster pistol to the ground and stalked off. "The hell with it!" he bellowed. "These inferior materials they have on Mongo! That would never happen on Earth with real steel. Damned inefficient miracle-makers in Arboria. Everything has to be made out of reconstituted wood. No wonder the damned blaster doesn't work."

Sari watched Zarkov stomp away and leaned quickly over to pick up the abandoned blaster pistol. She tucked it into her stretch waistband and hastened to catch up with Zarkov. She glanced back once. Neither Slan nor Brod stirred.

She breathed a sigh of relief.

CHAPTER 19

The tiny inn nestled under an enormous stand of giant bear's-paw fern. In front a sign depicting a large stag hung from the gable of a small shingled structure. Below it appeared the words:

THE STAG'S HORN

As Zarkov and Sari approached from the shelter of the ferns, they heard the sound of laughter.

They entered a small but cheery interior. At one end of the room a plank bar stretched across the wall. Square tables were spaced out in the center of the main room, with booths to one side. The floor was strewn with sawdust.

A group of men in leather tunics and homespun doublets underneath were seated at the largest table, drinking mugs of mead. They were big men with ruddy faces and huge, scarred hands, obviously woodsmen who held the fern concession to Prince Barin's Palace Wood Preserve.

They fell silent as Zarkov and Sari entered.

A big man, almost as wide as he was tall, stumbled out from behind the bar, wearing a sleeveless doublet with a soiled apron tied around his ample waist. He wore soft ankle boots. He had red hair and blue eyes and a round, laughing face.

"Welcome!" he cried. "Welcome to The Stag's Horn!"

Zarkov waved his hand. "Greetings."

"Sit ye down," the innkeeper said, waving to a corner table.

Sari and Zarkov sat down quietly. "Mead," Zarkov said. "Mead," Sari said. They waited while the innkeeper drew the mead from a barrel behind the bar and brought the two mugs over to them. The woodsmen at the next table were silent, two of them staring at Sari with puzzled eyes. Finally they began a low-voiced conversation, and turned from both Zarkov and Sari.

"Do you have a laserphone?" Sari asked the fat man.

"Aye," he said. "In me back room. Where be ye calling?"

Sari looked at Zarkov. Then she said, "The capital."

"Arboria?" He nodded. "Certainly. The laser rod is clear. Somebody called through yesterday."

Sari rose. "May I use it?"

"Aye," said the innkeeper. "I'll charge ye for the call. Have the operator put Innkeeper Gumm on the tab, if ye will."

Sari nodded. She walked off with Gumm and went through a plank door into another room.

Zarkov glanced around the interior of the inn. As he sat there drinking, he looked up to see one of the woodsmen detach himself from the table nearby and move quickly over to him. Looking around furtively, the woodsman, a youngster in his early twenties, sat down next to Zarkov and leaned toward him.

"Zarkov, isn't it?"

Zarkov's eyes widened. "Maybe."

"Maybe, nothing! You're Zarkov." The forester did not have a forest accent.

"And you?"

"Pabl."

"Okay. So?"

"They don't know I'm on patrol. I told them I thought you were my uncle. If any of them asks, remember." Pabl's eyes were hard. He was a lean-faced youth with dark eyes and dark hair that reached to his shoulders. He had a handsome, smooth-complexioned face with a very light mustache.

"All right," Zarkov said.

"You've come from the capital?"

"Yes."

"Going back?"

"Trying to."

"Good. We're working a big fern preserve not far from here. I can't leave the gang. And I can't use the laser-

99

phone without raising their suspicions. It would blow my cover. I need a courier to the capital."

Zarkov was amused. "You're an agent?"

"Yes. Prince Barin's intelligence. You know the prince. Of course you do, you're Zarkov. Now, listen carefully, there's a great deal to tell."

Zarkov nodded. "You recognize me. That's obvious. You seem authentic. I can only say I'll carry on your information if I know it's valid."

Pabl frowned. "It's a wild story, but it has to be told. Prince Barin must know. There's a secret army in the woods on its way to overthrow the capital."

Zarkov started. He thought of the blue men. He thought of what Sari had said about the secret army of Ming's they were looking for. He decided to play it dumb and see what Pabl had to say. "Who's behind it?"

"Ming," Pabl said. "At least, that's what I think. It's not at all clear exactly who is running it."

"So?"

Pabl glanced over his shoulder at his companions. One of them waved a hand at him and grinned, flicking mead foam from his mustache. Pabl laughed and waved back.

"I was topping a giant sword fern three days ago out of sight of the others," Pabl said in a low voice. "I finished the work and climbed down on my safety belt and jumped to the ground. As I walked over to the piece of downed timber to mark it for stripping, I suddenly saw that the fern fronds had fallen on something that was still alive."

"Something?" Zarkov frowned.

"It looked like a man," Pabl confessed. "I crawled under the fern fronds—those giant ferns are huge and extremely heavy—and pulled out a man. He was unconscious, but not dead. However, he was bleeding badly and had a broken arm."

"What was he doing there?" Zarkov asked, trying to keep his voice low.

"It wasn't so much what he was doing there, it was what he was," Pabl said softly.

"What was he?" Zarkov's voice was loud.

Pabl glanced at the other table and smiled. Several of the woodsmen had glanced up, but then they all turned away and began talking again amongst themselves.

100

"He was human," said Pabl, "but like nothing I've ever seen before. His skin was blue, bright blue, and he had scales on his skin. His eyes were yellow. Cat's eyes!" Pabl stared into Zarkov's face. "You don't believe me, do you?"

"I didn't say that, did I?"

"No, but—" Pabl paused. "I never told the others," he whispered. "Not because they wouldn't believe me, but because of what the man said."

"What did he say?"

"I tried to put the arm in a splint, but I apparently was too rough on him. Anyway, I didn't know then that he was more badly injured than I had supposed."

"Where is he now?"

Pabl ignored the question. "He told me the darndest story I've ever heard."

"Well?"

"The blue man told me that he was trying to escape and he begged me to hide him from his own people."

"His own people? Who are they? Where do they come from?"

"He said Cerulea. I never heard of the place. According to him, it's on Mongo somewhere. I couldn't get the details out of him. He was too badly hurt. And he said he and the others in Cerulea were all under the strict control of Ming the Merciless."

Zarkov nodded. "I know him. He's bad people."

"He said the other blue men were all just like him. It's some kind of secret army, raised by Emperor Ming to mount an attack on the capital and overthrow Prince Barin."

"What else did he say?"

"He told me about the blue men." Pabl glanced across the room, but no one paid any attention to them. "Some scientists of Ming's had been working for years on selective breeding. You know, chromosome matching and all that kind of thing."

"I know," Zarkov snapped. "What is this all about?"

"Well, the scientists had worked out a method of selective breeding years back, and had been applying it to a race of super warriors. Anyway, that was what the blue man called it. Incidentally, his name was Klab. Klab said that he was brought up in a secret colony called Cerulea, not far from Mingo, which had been isolated entirely from the rest of Mongo for many years. There scientists continue to work on selective breeding and utopian societies. A lot of the work is done by computers, Klab said."

"Go on. What about the blue men?"

"Well, the blue men are a genetically selected breed of men who are completely engineered for fighting."

"But why the blue color?"

Pabl's face lighted up. "You do believe me, then?"

"I'm simply listening to your story and judging," Zarkov replied, his voice rising. "Now get along with it."

"The indigo tint was selected for night forays. Tests show that such a skin color cannot be seen in the darkness of Mongo, particularly in the fifth moon of Mongo with its orange sheen."

Zarkov nodded. "I see. The blue skin and the cat's eyes."

"Right. The cat's eyes were especially selected since they could see in the dark as well as in the light. Klab had huge canines, too, and pointed molars. I forgot to tell you that."

"I see."

"Well, this experiment was kept entirely secret by Ming's scientists. For thirty years they continued and finally a large enough army was gathered together in the secret colony of Cerulea to try to mount an attack on Ming's traditional enemy—Arboria and the forest kingdom."

"And none of this leaked out?"

"No," Pabl said. "I never heard of it. And Klab said it was kept strictly confidential."

"You mean, Klab was brought up with these other warriors since birth to fight?"

"Right. These blue men have been bred to take orders, to carry them out, and to kill their enemies."

"What weapons do they use?"

"That's another thing," Pabl said. "They don't need weapons. They're born with weapons. Their fingernails."

"Fingernails!" Zarkov cried.

"Right. The hands seem completely normal. But when Klab unsheathed his nails, they became long talons exactly

102

like those of a cat. And they can rip and tear exactly like a cat's claws."

Zarkov moistened his lips. He and Sari had been very lucky not to go up against the two of them without the blaster pistol.

Zarkov moistened his lips. "So they don't need weapons."

"Right," said Pabl. "They're led by a fiendish general who is directly responsible only to Ming the Merciless. He's in complete charge of the operation. Each man has been bred and programmed for life to obey him and to do his bidding. The operation can only succeed, Zarkov. Believe me."

"What made this Klab turn against them?"

"Well, that's exactly it. You see, he was trying to escape from them when he was caught under the trees I was topping."

"What made him turn against them?" Zarkov repeated.

"He said that even though he had been bred and brainwashed throughout his youth, he and some of the others had managed to sneak in reading material from the outside world—which would be the rest of Mongo—and they had hungered to find out about the other life, where there were women living freely."

"Women?" Zarkov remembered Captain Slan's morbid interest in Sari.

"Yes. These are normal men, you see. But having been brought up in a military atmosphere all their lives, they had met only women sent from the Palace of Ming, cast-off harem girls sent out on order to be their temporary companions. They had never known any family life of any kind. No mother. No father. Just the test tube."

"I see."

"And so when they finally were sent on their mission— this was only a week ago—some of them had tried to test their freedom by escaping. But their leaders rounded them all up and killed them."

Zarkov sighed. "It's a grim story. Where is the defector now?"

Pabl sighed. "Klab? Klab is dead."

"Dead?" Zarkov blinked.

"I didn't know it, but he had internal injuries. When I

tried to help him to his feet, he collapsed, and then hemorrhaged until he was dead. I could do nothing for him. He wanted to come over to our side and warn our people," Pabl said softly.

Zarkov nodded. "What did you do with the body?"

"I buried him so the blue men wouldn't find him."

"Good thinking," Zarkov said, slapping him on the back.

"I've got to get back to my companions," Pabl said worriedly. "Will you carry the news to the capital?"

"I will," Zarkov said, and Pabl got up.

A piercing scream sounded from the other room. Zarkov recognized the sound of Sari's voice. He rose quickly, knocking the square table over, dashing the mugs of mead to the floor where they shattered.

"Help me!" Sari screamed.

Zarkov hurried across the room to the plank door, where Sari had left with the innkeeper. He tugged at the leather thongs. The door was blocked somehow.

"Sari! Are you in there?" he bellowed.

The woodsmen at the table were all staring toward him.

"Sari!" he boomed out.

He yanked on the thongs and the door jiggled in the frame. Suddenly Zarkov moved back, raised his booted foot, and smashed at the door. It splintered.

He ran into the other room quickly, the door sagging on its leather hinges behind him. The fat innkeeper was standing in the middle of the room, his hands tied in front of his fat belly, his face white with fear.

Sari was sagging against a tall man who held her tightly in his arms, looking at Zarkov over her shoulder. Her stretch blouse had been ripped at the shoulder. Blood seeped from a long wound there. The wound resembled a scratch from an enormous cat.

Lieutenant Brod grinned at Zarkov, with his hand at Sari's throat, ready to rip out her jugular with the bright-yellow hooked claws which Zarkov could now see unsheathed and in plain sight.

"Well, Zarkov?" Brod gurgled in that strange way of his.

Zarkov grabbed for his blaster pistol. He remembered only at that moment that he had thrown it down in the forest. He remembered seeing Sari go back and pick it up. He wondered why she had not been able to use it on Lieutenant Brod.

A hand shot out of the darkness at his side, gripping his upper arm tightly. Zarkov turned, startled. He found himself face to face with Captain Slan, whose yellow eyes gleamed with mirth.

"We meet again, Dr. Zarkov. You'll kindly refrain from any token opposition, if you please. Nothing will avail you succor this time." Slan chuckled. "Make up your mind, Dr. Zarkov, that you're going to come along with us to our detention chambers while the attack on the forest-kingdom's capital gets under way." Slan's yellow eyes gleamed. "Oh, as for that blaster pistol you seem so fond of, your shapely young friend has turned it over to us in mint condition." Slan reached in his cloak and drew it out, showing it to Zarkov with a sadistic leer. "Now, if you'll just come along with us."

"Hands off me, you miserable mutant!" Zarkov growled in his throat.

The sharp claws stabbed painfully into Zarkov's wrist. Blood seeped out onto his skin.

Captain Slan threw back his head and roared with laughter. Zarkov was aware of the yellow tongue flicking saliva off the blue lips.

Sari screamed again and Zarkov watched Slan thrust his blaster pistol negligently into the gilded belt around his yellow-and-orange doublet.

CHAPTER 20

For a moment, Kial stared in disbelief through the magniscopic sights of the laser-rod antimatter ray gun. He could not believe the superway was once again empty.

"Where did they go?" he howled.

Lari looked startled. "Where did who go?"

"Gordon and Arden," Kial snapped. "Look for yourself. They aren't there any more."

Lari put his eye to the magniscopic sights and adjusted the focus. "There's nobody there."

"Well, they were there a minute ago," Kial said angrily. "Now you've lost them again."

"I haven't lost them," Lari protested. "You've lost them."

"I can't understand it," Kial shouted, putting his eye again to the eyepiece and fiddling with the focusing lever. "You've got it all out of focus, dummy."

Lari stood with his hands on his hips. He stared through the wooded growth between the ray gun and the superway. "Well, I can't see them from here, either," he said at last. "They've gone, Kial. You were looking through the magniscope. Where did they go?"

"I don't know!" Kial screamed. "This mission is cursed, Lari. It's bewitched."

"Maybe they took a walk into the woods."

"That's about the stupidest thing I've ever heard, even from you."

"To look at the ferns, maybe. The forest is a beautiful sight, you know. Or maybe they wanted to watch the birds."

Kial spat in his anger. "Watch the birds! Come on, dummy. We've got to find them. Heap those branches over the ray gun. We can't take it with us and we don't want them finding it."

Lari sighed. "Yes, Kial." He looked up after he had thrown an armload of fern fronds on the laser gun. "Where are we going to look for them?"

Kial's eyes gleamed. "We'll use a little hunting savvy, Lari. Spoors."

"Spoors?" Lari repeated. "Oh. Footprints, you mean?"

"Or other tracks," Kial said. "Come on."

They picked up the prints alongside the superway where Flash and Dale had gone to look at the milestone. Lari spotted the milestone and walked around it to read the writing on the other side.

"Hey, Kial, look. It says, 'Flash and Dale—the answer is this way.'"

Kial stared at the message. "Who wrote that?" he asked in astonishment.

"I don't know."

Kial stared at the arrow and then followed the arrow through the forest growth. "Lari," Kial whispered, his face paling. "Do you know where that arrow is pointing?"

"Sure. To the answer. It says so here."

"Dummy! I mean it points right to the Tempendulum. That's where it points."

"The Tempendulum!" Lari repeated, his eyes fearful. "You mean they're going to find the Tempendulum?"

"Yes, dummy, unless we stop them," Kial yelled. "Now, come on, let's get moving. We haven't a moment to lose."

At the edge of the clearing where the Tempendulum had been built, Kial and Lari paused and crouched in the foliage, peering through the fern fronds at the big metallic dome.

"They're inside," Kial said mournfully. "They'll guess what it is. What are we going to do now?"

Lari jumped up and started across the clearing.

"Stop, dummy!" Kial yelped, reaching out and grabbing Lari by the belt. "Come back here, you moron. They'll see you."

"But—"

Kial drew him back into the shelter of the giant ferns. They both crouched there, peering out at the clearing.

"Well, now," said Kial. "We've got to figure out something. Gordon has discovered the Tempendulum and it won't take him long to do something about it."

"Then what?"

Kial's eyes lighted up. "Of course! We knock him out, and put him and Dale into the astro-seats, and pull the master switch on the Tempendulum. That throws them out into open time and they're lost forever in eternity!"

"Huh?" Lari said.

"I said—" Kial stopped and glared at Lari. "Oh, shut up and let me think."

"Look," Lari whispered after a moment.

Kial peered over Lari's fat shoulder. He saw Flash Gordon and Dale Arden inside the Tempendulum, moving back and forth and examining the instrumentation and the

107

pendulum hanging from the ceiling of the time dome. Once Kial thought he saw Flash Gordon look out the port directly toward them.

They heard the two Earthlings talking.

"It looks like some kind of pendulum to me, Flash," the girl's voice said.

"Quiet!" Kial whispered. "Listen. We can hear what they say."

Flash Gordon's voice said, "Pendulum. An old-fashioned pendulum, the kind of swinging weight that used to make grandfather clocks go before digital readouts and solid-state transistor packs. Dale, do you suppose—?"

"What, Flash?"

"Do you suppose this thing has anything to do with time-travel?"

Kial stared at Lari in horror. "He's guessed!" Kial hissed in despair.

"It might have, Flash," the girl said. "Look. If you read those letters on the console dials, it might mean Time Control. But I don't know what V.E. stands for. Or E.T.Z."

"Son of a gun!" Flash cried. "I think you're right. And if that's the case, what is that floating globe of heat and light?"

"I have no idea, Flash. But I'll bet. . . ." Dale's voice faded out.

"Wait a minute!" Flash said loudly. "Time-control! Of course! That refers to those belts Lari and Kial used. If those were time-travel belts, the two of them would vanish before our eyes if they traveled either forward or backward in time, wouldn't they?"

"Yes!" Dale exclaimed.

"And Arboria would vanish if it were made to travel in time, wouldn't it?"

"I don't know, Flash."

"Maybe not," Flash admitted. "It's a kind of farfetched idea. Still, perhaps there is some connection we can't see just now."

"What's that floating globe?"

"No idea. Something to do with light and energy. I suppose it's connected in some way to the pendulum."

Dale shrugged.

"Look at this, Dale. These dials are calibrated in years, decades, centuries. Obviously, the pendulum has something to do with the speed of time or of time itself. And those two people came to us—" Flash hesitated. "This metallic alloy, Dale, no wonder I've never seen it before. It's something from the future. Don't you see? Just like our two friends with the ray gun are from the future!"

"Of course," Dale replied.

"Look. I'm going to see if I can dismantle this pendulum. I think it must have something to do with the instrumentation on the console."

"Be careful, Flash," Dale said warningly.

"You stay over there," Flash instructed her. "Keep out of the way. I don't want anything to happen to you. On second thought, maybe you'd better get out of the dome while I work on that pendulum."

"I don't think you should, Flash."

"Nonsense. Don't worry about me. Now you get out of here and I'll take the pendulum apart."

Kial saw Dale Arden step out through the port into the sunshine. He motioned to Lari for silence; Dale did not look into the woods at all. She kept her eyes on Flash, working inside the hemispheroid.

"What's going to happen when he takes that pendulum apart?" Lari asked in a hushed voice.

"I don't know, but I've got a good idea what to do to the girl," Kial whispered back. "We'll sneak up on her, grab her, and hold her. When Gordon comes to the port, I'll knock him out and then we'll have him!"

"Kill him?" Lari asked.

"I've got a better idea," Kial said. "We'll do what we said before. We'll put him away for good. In time!"

Dale did not hear the two of them sneak up on her. When Kial reached out and caught her throat in the crook of his elbow, she was too startled to even cry out. She struggled for a moment, kicking back at him with her heels. But Kial did not let her go. With Lari's help, he pulled her away from the Tempendulum port and carried her into the woods.

"Flash!" Dale screamed, trying to attract his attention.

But her voice was so stifled by Kial's grip on her throat that she could not be heard.

Lari gagged her with a handkerchief, which he drew from his pocket, and quickly bound her hands behind her with a piece of duraflex cord. Then he tied her ankles and threw her down on the ground.

Kial tiptoed over to the Tempendulum and looked inside through the port. He could see Flash at work on the heart-shaped weight at the bottom of the pendulum. He now held it in his hands and was examining it carefully.

"Doesn't seem to be anything here, Dale," he said thoughtfully, turning his head.

"That's your tough luck, Gordon." Kial grinned, stepping over the sill of the port and advancing on Flash. Quickly, Flash stood up and tossed the heavy weight directly at Kial.

"If it's yours, take it!"

Kial tried to duck, but the heavy weight caught him in the stomach and knocked him down. He saw stars for a moment. He pushed aside the weight and got to his knees, waiting for Flash to attack.

Flash came at him, his hands extended in stiff karate fashion, moving up and down and measuring Kial's neck. Kial slowly came to his feet and leaped at Flash. Flash danced aside and gave him a stiff chop on the temple.

Quickly Kial pulled back, grabbing Flash's two wrists, and pulled him down to the floor of the dome, where he went back on his shoulders, and flipped completely over, sending Flash hurtling through the air over his head to slide on the floor toward the wall.

Flash leaped up and ran back to grab Kial's shoulders and pull him off the floor, jabbing him in the stomach with his knee at the same time.

"Oof!" Kial groaned.

Quickly, Flash chopped with his left fist at Kial's chin, jerking his head back hard. Following that with a right uppercut, Flash then pounded his left fist into Kial's stomach, then his right, and then his left again.

Kial dropped like a dead fish.

Pain started at Flash's neck and spread all through him.

He went down next to Kial.

He did not even see Lari behind him drop the tree

branch onto the floor. He had used it to club Flash on the skull.

Flash tried to get up, but could not. He hung there, staring at the floor, remembering that it was made from some strange metal alloy he had never seen before. He thought of time and the pendulum and he was suddenly floating in a void.

CHAPTER 21

Flash Gordon was seated in the astro-chair. He could see the hemispheroidal structure all around him. A queer violet light suffused the atmosphere. A high-pitched whining made the air shimmer everywhere. Tremendous surges of energy and power seemed to penetrate the atmosphere and enter his body.

He was unable to move.

Through the violet haze that grew all around him, he could see the fat man, Lari, seated at the console nearby. Lari glanced back over his shoulder at Flash, grinning an inane smile. With his hands he manipulated dials and levers on the console, all the while watching the astro-seat on which Flash was sprawled.

Now Flash saw that the heavy weight of the pendulum was deposited in his lap. It was tied to his body with some kind of strap. Another one of the substances that had come from the future? Obviously, yes.

Where was Dale?

Now, out of the corner of his eye, Flash saw Kial rise slowly from the floor of the hemispheroidal chamber to stare bleakly at him. He opened his mouth to speak, but the hum of the energy hurtling through the air about him made it impossible to hear what was being said.

Then Flash saw the floating ovate globe move over his

own head. It seemed to be the source of the humming and trembling.

"I got him in the astro-seat," Lari said proudly from the console. Flash knew he was talking to Kial.

"Good, good," Kial said. "Pull the master switch and send him into eternity."

"Exactly what I was going to do, Kial," Lari chortled, and reached out his hand to pull the largest of the switches in front of him.

The noise in the air increased around Flash. He felt the heart-shaped weight tied to his stomach suddenly move against his flesh. The hollow globe in the air spun erratically. Then the violet haze all around him turned to a kind of rainbow kaleidoscope of colors flashing from one end of the dome to the other and back again.

"Dale!" Flash cried. "Where are you?"

There was no answer.

Lari laughed through the hazy rainbowlike obscurity, but Flash could no longer see him. "He thinks she's with him."

"Maybe we should have sent her with him to—"

That was all Flash heard. It was Kial's voice, but it suddenly faded away.

The rainbow colors grew in intensity until Flash saw nothing else. Then the light seemed to speed up, and it was as if he were captured in the light itself and hurtled through the air and into space.

There was no dome around him now.

He shot through open air and endless waste. There was absolutely nothing around him except the astro-seat and the heart-shaped weight against his stomach. The weight was turning over and over and he was turning over and over with it, and the astro-seat simply clung to his back. Or so it seemed.

Now he was out onto the edges of eternity, with distance absolutely infinite. He saw strange bursts of light millions of miles away, and then dazzling displays of exploding stars and planets and novas in the throes of creation. Lightning in chains and in strange shapes flashed across the sky all around him, but never touched him.

He was stunned and his body felt as if it were in total shock, perhaps in a state of arrested animation like a man

112

might feel being electrocuted by one of Earth's old-fashioned electric chairs.

Through what might have been centuries he hurtled and then, suddenly, he realized that he hung suspended over a strange and ghastly sight. He looked down from the astro-seat, which hung in the air over what seemed to be a blighted landscape of some kind. Flash was reminded of deserts and dying lakes and dead seas he had seen on Earth during the pollution crisis before the World Council took over the management of the ecology.

Yes, he was looking down on a dying planet! The ground was seared and cracked. Not a living plant was in sight. Sand and clay and volcanic effluvia predominated. There was no atmosphere, only a stillness like that which surrounded the astronauts from Earth who had finally landed on Earth's moon in the past.

Then he saw buildings in the distance. The buildings were standing, but were beginning to decay. Bricks had fallen out of the walls. No windows were unbroken. Pieces of rotten wood lay about the bottoms of the buildings like detritus from a falling mountain.

Huge cracks seamed the dried-out loam. Into the cracks, rocks and pebbles drifted, although there was no wind to be seen and nothing to be blown by the wind except dust and sand. A poisonous mist hovered over the surface of the terminated planet.

And then the mist shifted and Flash saw a strange sight in the sky. It was the seventh of Mongo's suns, the last of them all. Like the other six, it was also in its death throes. Gaseous vapors swirled about its silhouette, sparkling with some kind of eternal fire, and vanished into the void as the heat of the sun went in the last of the fires. Auras of strange pastel light emanated from the sun as the last of its vapors were slowly consumed by the diminishing scraps of its heat.

Soon it would be a cold satellite hurtling through space—a meteor without fire. And Mongo would go with it, a dead planet with no future but eventual disintegration.

"It has to be Mongo," Flash said. "I must have jumped thousands of years into the future! Thousands! Lari must have thrown me ahead as far as he could. I'm trapped out here in eternity. There's no place to go now."

Then suddenly mist swept around him, lights flashed, and his body went numb again. . . .

For what seemed forever, the surging power sped through him. He moved in space again and then the lights faded from the vastness of the distances about him and he saw the planet below him. But this time it was shrouded in a gray mist.

He peered through the mists and they cleared enough for him to see the scene below. He was in a swamp of some kind—or rather he was suspended above it in the astro-seat. It was a swamp of algae and water plants from a long-ago era. As he watched, he saw strange reptilian monsters pushing through the mud and the goo, foraging for food.

An enormous, ponderous-looking creature like a dinosaur was locked in mortal combat with another like a pterodactyl, thrashing about in the swamp water that was now turning red with blood. A miasma of foul odors rose from the surface of the swamp, engulfing Flash and forcing him to close his eyes.

A tremendous explosion sounded. In the distance, Flash saw a cloud of smoke and lava belch into the skies. Molten lava rock hurtled through the air, red hot and sizzling loudly as the pieces fell into the swamp. Sulphurous smoke swirled up around him. Hot ash singed his clothing.

The air turned to fire. Smoke billowed up around him. The dinosaur bellowed and struck out at the pterodactyl for the final stroke, and then sank into the muddy waters and died. Blood gurgled to the surface. The pterodactyl bellowed a chant of victory and turned to slosh away in the foul water.

Its triumph was short-lived. An enormous cloud of molten lava, glowing red and yellow as it whirled through the air, caught the water just in front of the beast, sending a boiling geyser of steam into the air, and the pterodactyl screeched in agony as it was boiled alive in the lava-roiled water.

Flash turned his head.

And then he was moving again.

"Hey!" he said aloud. "I've gone back in time, all the way to the beginning. How about that? And now it looks as if I'm heading for the future again."

The violet light closed in around him. . . .

When the haze cleared, Flash saw that he had gone into the future. He saw a very clean-looking city below him— tall towers, multi-leveled roadways, trees and parks staggered throughout the industrialized area for ecological balance, clean air, sparkling water in rivers nearby, green forests all around.

"Beautiful place," Flash murmured.

He saw a large square in the center of the city, a statue in the middle dominating the square.

"Wonder who the hero is?" Flash said. "Maybe it's Prince Barin or someone else we know."

Then he was swinging closer to the statue, so close that he could see it very clearly. And it seemed very strange to him, almost as if he were looking into an enormous mirror. The head of the statue looked exactly like his own head!

He stared.

The monument on which the statue stood said the following:

FLASH GORDON
THE MIGHTY LIBERATOR
OF ANCIENT MONGO

And he saw that the statue was a metallic representation of himself. He was in his uniform, holding a gigantic sword in his hand, quite like a conquistador of some earlier Earth culture rather than a conqueror of Mongo. But, nevertheless, the spirit of victory was there. The statue was dedicated to Flash Gordon.

There was more:

CHAMPION OF FREEDOM AND JUSTICE
DEFENDER OF THE OPPRESSED AND
CRUSADER AGAINST ALL TYRANTS.

"It's a statue of me," he said in astonishment. "Must be

115

hundreds of years in the future. How did I become a legend? Or maybe it's not me. Maybe it's my son or grandson or great-grandson."

The mists closed around him again. . . .

The planet was filled with mist and then it became clear again. He felt himself moving, and then slowing down almost to a complete stop. He felt that he could almost rise from the astro-seat. The enormous weight of the heart-shaped thing in his lap seemed like nothing now.

Was the time-trip through?

No.

He was in the forest kingdom, or what looked greatly like it.

He could see the metallic dome down there in the woods—what Kial and Lari called the Tempendulum. He was hovering over the place he had been, but now he guessed he was very far in the future, for the two military men he saw were dressed exactly like Kial and Lari. He could see that the two men were not Kial and Lari, however.

And then, to his shock, he could see a third man quite clearly.

The third man was Emperor Ming!

Flash stared. How could Ming be in the future? Perhaps it was Ming's machine, and then—

No! It was not Ming. He could tell by the voice.

The creature who looked like Ming said: "All right, Orto and Lanl. You have your orders. See that you do not fail!"

One of the royal police bowed briefly. "Yes, Great Ming XIII. We hear and we obey. But we must be sure before we obey."

"Sure of what?" Ming XIII demanded.

Ming XIII, thought Flash. That's what he is—a descendant of Ming the Merciless.

"Forget all this nonsense," Ming said. "The Tempendulum will carry you to any moment of the past you want. We've already gone through the details on the computers. Now get in there, set the dials, and be off with you."

"But you must promise us that Flash Gordon will not interfere! It is written—"

116

"I've promised you that!" Ming XIII said impatiently.
"We're sending another time probe to take care of him.
Now you get in there and strap yourself into the astro-
seats."

"We obey, Ming XIII," one of the men cried.

"Remember," Ming warned, "get Prince Barin at any
price. The other probe will take care of Gordon. You
need not worry."

"Yes, Mighty Ming XIII," said the other man.

Flash sat up in the astro-seat. "That's what it's all
about! Ming is sending back assassins to kill Prince Barin
in Arboria. I've got to stop them. And Kial and Lari—
they were sent to take care of me so the other two could
kill Prince Barin."

Flash lifted the heart-shaped weight and started to jump
out of the astro-seat.

The heavens were full of light and energy and Flash
could not move. A numbness crept into his arms and legs
and he sank back into the seat.

"I can't get up," he cried. "I'm moving again—across
time. I've missed the chance to stop them."

The two uniformed men of Ming XIII's royal police
climbed into the Tempendulum as the mists closed in
around Flash and he began his trip through space and
time once again.

CHAPTER 22

Dale lay on her side on the ground and watched Lari
walk toward the Tempendulum. She could hear a great
deal of noise inside the hemispheroidal building. It sounded like the humming of some giant transformer or electromagnetic generator.

Quickly she wriggled around to see if she could touch
her ankles with her hands. Lari had bound her wrists be-

hind her. By bending her knees, she could touch her feet with her hands. She tugged at the tight knot he had tied in the duraflex twine. It was strong, unbreakable cord, but the knots were not pulled too snugly for her fingers. She had always prided herself on her athletic ability, anyway. Now she thanked her good muscle tone for the dexterity of her fingers.

She heard Lari and Kial talking in the Tempendulum. One of them laughed loudly. They were doing something to Flash. Dale wondered if they might not be trying to put him into one of those astro-seats. She could see them moving about through the entry port.

"There!" she said. "I'm free!" She shed the pieces of cord and ran over to the port, looking into the huge hollow dome. She saw Flash seated in one of the astro-chairs, unconscious, the enormous heart-shaped object that had been attached to the bottom of the pendulum tied to his stomach by a leather belt.

Lari stood at the huge console of instruments. Kial stood by Flash, a wicked leer on his face.

"Good, good," Kial said eagerly. "Pull the master switch and send him into eternity!"

"Exactly what I was going to do, Kial!" Lari answered. And he threw the big master switch at the console.

There was a movement of air inside the dome, and the floating ovate globe suddenly glowed bright purple. Dale drew back. She could feel the heat emanating from it. And then the weight in Flash's lap vibrated, throwing the atmosphere around it into a kind of convulsion. Instantly the interior of the dome turned a luminescent violet— quite similar to the violet ray created in a radioactive substance.

Lari cackled loudly. Kial turned to the console and grinned. Both pointed to the astro-seat where Flash sat.

He had vanished! Dale recoiled, her hand over her mouth, her eyes wide with terror.

Flash and the astro-seat were no longer there. They had hurled him out into timeless eternity, into endless space where he would be unable to harm them.

"They'll do it to me if they catch me," Dale said. "I've got to get to Arboria. Only Doc Zarkov can help Flash now. If I can get there to see him, and if we can find the

Tempendulum again, he can get Flash back from outer space."

Dale turned and ran into the woods.

She was hidden behind the giant fern fronds when she heard a shout from the clearing outside the Tempendulum.

"Where's that fool woman?" Kial yelled.

"Huh? I tied her up. She can't have gone far."

"Dummy, you've let her escape."

Lari stumbled out through the entry port of the Tempendulum and looked around in a daze. "Yeah, she's gone."

"You bet your life she's gone."

Lari pointed to the ground where the two pieces of duraflex cord lay. "She got loose! She's a magician, that's what—a female wizard."

Kial grabbed Lari by the throat and started to shake him. "She's no wizard. You're a moron, that's all. She untied the granny knots you put in that cord. That's what happened. She's at large, now, and worse luck to us."

"We've got to find her," Lari declared.

"You bet your sweet life we have to." Kial paused. "She's not so important as Gordon, of course. She's just a silly woman. But we can't report in to Ming XIII that we let her get away. He's mad enough at us, anyway."

Dale moved quietly through the purple-and-orange foliage of the forest kingdom. She was seething with anger.

"Not important enough, am I? I'm just a woman, is that it? All right Mr. Kial and Mr. Lari, you two male chauvinists from the future, let's see how important I can be to you. If I get to Zarkov, I'll fix your little red wagons."

She pushed a bear's-paw fern over in her anger, and sprayed spores all around the loam. She ran.

Exhausted, Dale finally sank down onto a soft pad of semi-aquatic algae that grew from the forest floor. She had run into a huge stand of bladder ferns. The seventh sun of Mongo could not penetrate the forest of giant vegetation above her. She was alone. She was tired. She was frightened.

"Come on, girl," she said through clinched teeth. "This is no way to be. You don't know where that silly superway is, and you're lost. But if you press on, you'll certainly find

119

something soon. Arboria has simply got to be in that general direction."

She closed her eyes and tried to rest a moment.

"At least Kial and Lari couldn't pick up my tracks. I'd hear them if they had. They run like a pair of hippopotamuses."

She opened her eyes, and folded her arms across her chest. It was cool so deep in the ferny part of the forest kingdom. She looked around her. The enormously tall stalks of the bladder ferns cut down her vision considerably.

"What was that?"

Dale sat up straight, her hands pushing against the algae bed. She cocked her head to one side. Had she heard something? Was it Kial? Was it Lari? Had they picked up her trail in the woods?

No. It was the voice of a man. He did not have any familiar dialect. His words were spoken in a strange, almost artificial accent. It sounded like the kind of speech uttered by a person who had learned a language without ever having talked to anyone. It was, in short, a kind of programmed speech.

An android? Dale shivered. She had heard of no andies on Mongo. Unless that fiend Ming the Merciless had bought some from one of the outer planets in the system and shipped them in to do his dirty work. Still, she was sure Prince Barin and the General Council of Mongo would put a stop to that soon enough.

Dale rose and tiptoed through the woods toward the sound of the voice.

She saw two men.

Her heart stopped beating, then speeded up.

"God forbid!" she whispered. They had blue skins! Their complexions were blue and their eyes yellow!

But they spoke Mongolite with that peculiar artificial accent.

"Half an hour maybe," one said. "We'll be into Cerulea and in front of a good hot meal. I'm hungry enough to eat an eel!"

"What about the prisoners?" the other asked. "Do you anticipate any trouble with them?"

120

"The captain certainly doesn't think there'll be any trouble with that young woman."

The first giggled. "I hardly think I would have trouble with her, either."

"Nor I to tell the truth." A pause. "She's of the forest kingdom."

"Cute. Very luscious." A sigh. "The other?"

"They'll kill him. Or wire him to the main computers. He's a brain where he came from, they tell me."

"Oh?"

"Head of the science laboratory in Arboria."

Dale felt a chill race along her backbone. Dr. Zarkov was head of the science laboratory in Arboria. Had they captured him? And what was that about wiring him into the computer?

Dale crept forward.

Now she could see the two men more plainly. They were definitely blue-fleshed with yellow eyes. They wore brilliant red cloaks over doublets of yellow and orange. The effect was a dazzling one, a combination that made the colors and shapes vibrate before her eyes, especially against the lavender and orange of the bladder-fern foliage in back of them.

The two men puffed on rolled leaves of some kind. Dale smelled a sticky sweet aroma like cannabis sativa. Perhaps it was an allied genus.

"Let's get back," one of the men said.

The other nodded, stubbing out his burning stick, and the two of them made off through the dense woods.

Dale followed them.

And there, in a small clearing not far off, she found Dr. Zarkov and a girl dressed in hunter's green, both tied to the stalk of a bladder fern. Zarkov was grumbling to himself and shaking his head with disgust. The girl's eyes darted here and there as if she were trying to figure someway out of the mess she and Zarkov were in.

I wish I could catch Doc Zarkov's eye, Dale thought. And then she had an idea.

She reached into her stretchsuit where she kept her bag, and brought it out. It was a most compact purse, one that did not even show an outline on her body, but in which she carried all the things she needed. Aspirin. Kelp pills.

121

Energy tablets. Heat cubes. Vitamins A through Q^1. Lipstick. Comb. Mirror.

She removed the mirror. It was very dark in the bladder-fern forest, but in the clearing a bit of light filtered down through the branches. She moved over toward the edge of the ferns, where she could just catch a glint of the light from Mongo's seventh sun. She tilted the mirror to deflect the rays into Zarkov's eyes.

He blinked and shook his head.

"What in hell is going on?" he boomed out, staring about angrily. "Get that light out of my eyes."

Dale saw a group of blue men standing about in the woods, smoking and munching on some compressed food stock. One of them laughed. But no one really saw the flash of light across Zarkov's beard.

Then Zarkov calmed. His eyes roamed the surrounding woods. He saw Dale. His eyes widened and then he winked briefly. A moment later he sagged against the fern and feigned sleep.

Now what? Dale wondered. Zarkov had seen her. And he had winked. He had some plan. What on Mongo was it?

Suddenly Zarkov jerked upright against the fern, his eyes wide, his beard bristling.

"A salamander!" he boomed out. "It's a salamander!"

One of the blue men turned to gaze at him contemptuously. "Shut up, Zarkov. Don't try any of your little games with me."

"Fool. I can hear those things from a distance!"

"How can you hear and we can't, Zarkov?" asked the blue man, who seemed to be the leader.

"Just trust me, Slan. I can hear. It was an experiment. I implanted an auditory amplifier in my aurical centers that would be activated by sound vibrations above those commonly audible to the human ear."

Captain Slan lifted an eyebrow. "And you claim you can hear the approach of a salamander now?"

"In the distance," Zarkov snapped. "You know how dangerous they are."

"We know the danger," Slan agreed. "But we know you, too. You are a liar of the most artful type, Dr. Zarkov. I simply don't believe you."

122

"Believe me," Zarkov pleaded, beginning to wrestle with his bonds. "Believe me. There's a giant salamander on its way here. Those animals can smell men for miles!"

A second blue man came up to the leader and whispered in his ear. The leader shook his head angrily.

"It's closer, Captain Slan," Zarkov said piteously, twisting about on the ground. "You've got to believe me. I'd run for my life, if I could. Nobody, not even the eight of us, could stand off one of those monsters."

A third blue man said, "Let's leave the two of them here, Captain. If he isn't lying, he and the girl will get theirs."

Dale ran back out of sight and picked up a large smooth stone that lay in the woods. She hurled it with all her might through the ferns. It hit one of the fronds with a loud smash and the sound echoed in the woods.

She picked up another, and threw it closer to the clearing where the blue men had Zarkov and the girl tied up.

"All right," Slan cried, staring into the darkened woods. "There's something there!" He turned to his men. "Leave the two of them here. And double-time into the woods." He pointed with his arm. "That way!"

The men moved out quickly.

Dale ran into the clearing and bent over Zarkov.

"Good girl, Dale," Zarkov cried. "You're a smart kid."

"You bet I am." Dale laughed. She turned to the girl's bonds and loosened them.

"Meet Sari, Dale. That's Dale Arden, Sari."

Sari said, "Hi."

"Doc," Dale said, "they've got Flash. You've got to help him."

"Where is he?" Zarkov asked.

"He's in the Tempendulum."

"What's that?" Zarkov frowned.

"A kind of time-travel dome."

Zarkov shrugged. "Well, then," he bellowed, "let's get out of here and go find Flash Gordon!"

Zarkov grabbed Dale's arm and Sari's, and started across the clearing.

The woods rustled.

The six blue men appeared, spread out, and surrounded

123

the three of them. Their yellow claws were extended out from their hands as they held them poised for attack.

Dale screamed.

"Very neat, Dr. Zarkov," Captain Slan said smoothly. "And that makes one more for the party back to Cerulea." He laughed. His yellow fangs showed. "The more the merrier is the way we say it in Cerulea, Dr. Zarkov."

"In Arboria we say you win one, you lose one," growled Zarkov.

CHAPTER 23

Now the violet haze cleared once again and Flash knew exactly where he was. He recognized the interior of the Spaceport Inn, where he had taken a room just after arriving by rocket from Earth with Dale. He saw himself asleep in the bed and he saw the man he now knew as Kial sneak into the room.

Flash felt the tremendous speed of the astro-seat as it slowed almost to a halt. He gripped the heart-shaped pendulum weight, but could not budge it from his lap. Instead, he watched.

He saw Kial reach for the blaster pistol holster hanging on the bedpost, and then he knew instantly what had happened.

"He took my blaster pistol and left me an empty holster," Flash said. "When I tried to use it on the superway later, I suddenly didn't have it. I only thought it vanished in my hand. I actually never did have it."

Then, as Kial stood there hanging the empty holster back on the bedpost, Flash saw his own figure rise from the bed and rush out at Kial. He saw Kial go through the open window and into the backyard. He saw the man struggle from the slop pit in the yard, and then Flash ran through the corridors of the inn, and Dale ran beside him.

He tried to move out of the chair, but he could not.
The violet light closed in on him. . . .

Then the astro-seat slowed down once again. He saw the mists clear and he was on the superway. The astro-seat was almost still now. He could not even feel the weight of the pendulum on his lap. He saw Kial and Lari, and he saw himself, in that earlier time with Dale.

He struggled against the force of inertia that gripped his muscles, and now, to his immense surprise and pleasure, he broke through the gravity barrier that seemed to have enveloped him as he sat supine in the chair.

He was out of the seat and running across the superway. He saw Kial and Lari menacing Flash and Dale. He saw Lari knock him down with the butt of the blaster pistol rather than risk zapping Kial with a straight shot. Then he saw Dale lean over him to try to revive him.

Lari pointed at Flash, and Flash shook his head and tried to rise from where he had fallen. But he could not. He fell back.

"He'll never get up," Kial snorted derisively.

"I don't like it, Kial," Lari said.

"Get on with it," Dale said defiantly. "If you're not going to use that blaster pistol, then give it to me."

Good for Dale, Flash thought.

Kial grinned. "You'd like that, wouldn't you, lady?"

Dale stared hard at him.

Flash ran up to the group on the roadway. "Now, now," he said. "Didn't your mother ever tell you not to play with guns?"

Dale stared at him. He saw her shock and surprise. He saw her look at the other Flash lying on the superway, trying to get up.

"Hey!" yelped Kial as Flash reached out and grabbed Kial's right hand, which held the blaster pistol.

"What is this," Kial cried, trying to turn around.

Lari gaped at Flash. "It's Gordon!"

"Gordon?" repeated Kial. Now he turned and stared in bewilderment at Flash. His hand opened and the blaster pistol fell to the pavement from the pressure of Flash's grip. "Gordon?"

Flash exerted more pressure on Kial's arms and twisted him around toward him.

"It's just like dancing," Flash said merrily. "I'd rather have a more attractive partner than you, but if it has to be you then it has to be you."

"Shut up!" cried Kial.

"You shut up!" Flash twisted Kial's arm in a hammer-lock and gripped him around the waist. "Now, get out of here and leave us in peace and quiet."

Perspiration ran down Kial's face. Flash spun him away. Kial staggered over into a heap on the pavement.

"Look out, Flash!" Dale cried. "It's Lari!"

Flash turned just in time to see Lari running at him, aiming the second blaster pistol. Flash slammed his fist into Lari's stomach.

"Oof!" Lari said. The blaster pistol fell away from him. He went down on his back.

"Dale," Flash called, "are you all right?"

"Yes," said Dale. "But how did you do that?"

"It's a long story," Flash began slowly.

Kial was crawling over the pavement. "Lari, let's get out of here quick!"

"Yeah," Lari said. "Right now!"

"Tell me," Dale said to Flash.

Now the pendulum once again exerted its irresistible force upon Flash. He opened his mouth to speak to Dale, but he could not hold himself away from the astro-seat. Impelled by a power greater than gravity and light, he was drawn forcibly back to the astro-seat, which waited in the mists rising around him.

He saw the blaster pistol lying on the pavement of the superway. Reaching down, he scooped it up and stuck it in his belt. Still moving, he glanced back to see Dale's puzzled face.

"Poor Dale," he said. "She looks so confused. I've got to tell her somehow! Maybe I can—"

He saw the milestone marking the distance from Arboria by the side of the roadway. Quickly he took out a pencil he carried and scratched a message on the stone:

FLASH AND DALE—THE ANSWER IS THIS WAY.

He finished the note off with an arrow pointing in the direction of the Tempendulum in the woods. That should give them a head start on Kial and Lari. And if they found the Tempendulum. . . .

Then he was in the astro-seat and the weight of the pendulum flung him once again through space as the violet mists closed in.

CHAPTER 24

It was a fairly large cell without openings of any kind except for the one barred entrance. The bars were made of annealed drogiron from ore mined on Mongo. Zarkov grasped the bars and shook them. The bars were solidly embedded in a metal doorframe.

Finally, he turned from the door and paced across the stone floor of the cell.

"Ten steps one way. Eight steps the other." He fumed. "A prison. Me, Zarkov, incarcerated!" He walked over to one of the walls and pounded his fists against it. "Klang rock. Too hard to drill through, even if we had a drill. Damn! To think that a fine mind like mine is chained here in a cage, while the fates of Arboria and the forest kingdom are being decided by that miserable indigo warmonger upstairs."

Dale sat up on the bare bunk that lined one wall. "Please, Doc, must you emote so?"

"Yes, I must emote so," Zarkov snapped, his voice vibrating. "Dammit! I came out of Arboria to find you and Flash. And since that time, all I've gotten into is trouble. My airscout crashes and sinks to the bottom of the Dismal Swamp. I'm joined by an agent of Barin's intelligence council. We're set upon by strange armies of blue humanoids bent on destroying the forest kingdom, obviously mercenaries in the employ of Ming the Merciless. And then through some idiocy we're brought here to Cerulea, where the monster and his gang of undesirables hang out."

Sari got up and walked back and forth. "Oh, come on, Dr. Zarkov. It isn't all over yet. We've got to get out of

127

here, that's all. I must report to Prince Barin before the blue men attack."

"You never did tell me what happened at the inn," Zarkov said curiously. "Was there a laserphone in the back room?"

"Oh, yes. But the moment I got there and punched in the call letters, that innkeeper grabbed me and held me until he could call for Captain Slan and that grimy Lieutenant Brod. They had just gotten there when you came in. And then they tied up the innkeeper, so he wouldn't demand payment for helping them."

Zarkov shook his head. "Selective breeding," he muttered. "I never would have believed it. Cat men. Claws. Blue skins. Yellow eyes. Ridiculous!" Zarkov snorted. "Yet, here they are, waiting to take over Arboria." Zarkov beat his fists against the wall again. "We've got to get out of here." He turned abruptly. "Dale, you say Flash is in some kind of time trap?"

Dale took a deep breath. "I've told you all that already, Doc. He disappeared before my eyes when one of those creeps who tried to kill us threw the master switch on that pendulum."

Zarkov stroked his beard. "Pendulum. It's a sure-fire manner of measuring time, all right, and of keeping time at a regular pace. Probably regulates the speed with which the time capsule operates, too." He frowned. "You say they strapped Flash into an astro-seat?"

"No. He just sat there. They put the weight of the pendulum in his lap."

Zarkov blinked his eyes. "And that floating globe?"

"Power, Doc. Light and heat and energy. All trapped inside a black opaque lining."

"Mmm ... interesting. We've got to get out of here. I want to see that thing. If, as you say, Flash is swinging back and forth in time, helpless to come back to the present, we've got to help him."

"That's why I wanted to find you," Dale said quietly.

"You found me. Tied up!" Zarkov smashed one fist into the other open palm. "Damn! This is intolerable. All the time Barin waits around there at the palace, ready to proclaim the anniversary of Arboria's independence, and this army of blue fiends is preparing to attack the city."

There was a moment's silence as Zarkov paced.

128

"That ray gun," he said to Dale. "Do you think these blue monsters are responsible for that?"

"I don't really know," Dale replied. "It's terribly powerful. I told you what it did to the suspension system of that jetcar you designed."

Zarkov waved his hand airily. "Yes, yes. Well, we've simply got to get out of here."

He ran to the barred door and shook it once again. "Out!" he screamed. "Out!" His voice echoed in the hollow stone corridors of the prison. "Out!"

He slumped on the bunk, depressed.

It seemed hours later before Captain Slan appeared. He was smiling and clean-shaven. His yellow eyes were bright in the flickering light from the dirty torches hanging in their wall niches.

He peered in through the bars. "Zarkov." He smiled broadly. "Come, we're going on a stroll through Cerulea."

Zarkov glanced at Dale and Sari. He winked. Then he turned to Slan. "It's about time. I don't mind telling you, I feel like I'm rotting away in this airless prison of yours."

Slan nodded. "Spunky one, aren't you?"

"Well! Aren't you going to let me out?"

A blue man with a set of keys appeared at Slan's side. Slan gestured to the lock on the barred door. The keeper of the keys bent over and inserted a metal key into the lock and turned it. The iron barred door swung inward.

Slan stood outside, smiling sardonically. "Aren't you coming out?"

Zarkov moved quickly, leaping for Slan's body, hurtling with his shoulder aimed for Slan's stomach, and wrapped his hands around the man's body. Slan grunted and kicked his knee, hitting Zarkov in the chest.

Zarkov leaned backward and cartwheeled back into the room, bringing the blue man with him. Slan cuffed at Zarkov, and grunted loudly in his exertions. Immediately, Sari and Dale leaped on the struggling men, grasping at Slan's red cloak.

Sari chopped at him with stiff hand motions.

Slan's claws tore Zarkov's battle jacket, but not his skin.

The keeper of the keys ran down the corridor, shouting.

Zarkov rushed out into the corridor, waving to the girls to follow. Sari gave Slan a push and he reeled backward, and smashed his head hard on the wall. Slowly he slumped down to the floor and lay there, unmoving.

Sari leaned over him. She felt the pulse. There was none. The man was dead.

Dale and Sari ran out after Zarkov. They were at the turning of the corridor when a portcullis of iron bars resembling the cell door fell suddenly from the ceiling, slamming down in the corridor and locking in place.

Zarkov grasped the bars and tugged, shouting insanely.

Beyond the bars, several blue men appeared, carrying torches. One of them was the second-in-command, who had been with Slan at the Stag's Horn Inn.

Lieutenant Brod grinned at Zarkov. "How interesting—Captain Slan was right."

Zarkov growled at him. "Your Captain Slan is dead. How do you like them apples?"

"Apples. Staple of an Earthling's diet," Brod said with a smile. "Slan is dead, you say?"

"Yes," Zarkov hissed. "We'd be out of here now if you hadn't dropped that damned portcullis on us."

"Slan may appear dead, but I assure you he is not," Brod said with a faint smile.

He moved forward and thrust his torch through the bars of the portcullis. Zarkov turned to stare behind him.

Captain Slan approached them with a sardonic and evil smile on his blue face. "One thing about selective breeding, Dr. Zarkov," he said smugly as he came up to the group cowering at the portcullis. "You can create a body that will almost instantly renew its own life, even if totally extinguished. You see, it's going to be rather hard to get rid of me. How do you like them rutabagas, Dr. Zarkov?"

"Rutabagas," Zarkov muttered.

"Oh, we have interesting langtapes here in Cerulea that we play in our sleep. We know a little bit about everything."

Zarkov sagged against the bars.

Dale bit her lip and Sari stood without moving.

"And now, Dr. Zarkov. If you'll come with me, I would like to show you exactly what we are doing in Cerulea. It will interest you greatly, I am sure."

They were cages, actually. Large cages built of drogiron. They were suspended from large wooden beams

130

that crossed the huge room at intervals of ten feet. Each was about the size of a small leopard cage. A trap door was built into the bottom of each. The floor below the cages was covered with a thick and very soft carpet.

The room contained twenty cages.

Now they were empty.

"The dormitory, Dr. Zarkov," Slan told him as they came in through the one entrance to the room.

Zarkov felt cold. "And the cages? What are they for?"

"They keep the inmates from attempting escape, murder, or, as a last resort, suicide."

"Suicide?"

"Oh, many attempt suicide. Before I thought of the cages, I used to keep them in very nice rooms. Drapes. Carpets. Vidscreens. All the comforts of home. As befitted a woman. But they strangled themselves on bathrobe cords, bedsheets, and similar sordid things. I simply had to move them to safer areas of concentration." Slan smiled. "Hence the cages."

"But who—?"

"We are men of the world, Dr. Zarkov," Slan said carefully. "Not for us the gilded cages. Not for us."

"The girls?" Zarkov gasped, his face turning pale.

"Exactly," Slan said with a smile. "With selective breeding of the warrior class, we do not waste time on the clothing, feeding, and the training of women. Naturally, we bring them in from outside. An occasional kidnapping. A girl lost in the woods, that kind of thing. Don't worry. Dale Arden and Sari will not be all that unhappy."

Zarkov exploded. "You're a monster, Slan. Do you know that?"

Slan smiled. "And those who are especially favored are sent to Ming the Merciless, there to lead the life of a princess of the royal harem. What could be sweeter, Dr. Zarkov?"

"Unspeakable!" Zarkov boomed angrily.

Captain Slan leaned against the wall of the enormous laboratory and folded his arms across his chest. With his crimson cloak, his yellow eyes, and the fangs of his yellow teeth showing against his blue face, he was the representation of the devil incarnate.

Zarkov shivered.

"And this will also interest you, Dr. Zarkov. It's our laboratory. The finest one on Mongo, actually. No one knows about it except Ming and us. This is the largest and most complex computer in the universe, Dr. Zarkov."

Zarkov nodded. He looked over the banks of teletype keys, readout ports, blinking lights, and whirring reels of tape turning clockwise and then counterclockwise in monotonous rhythm. There must have been forty computer blocs, all arranged in two rows, both facing an aisle down which Captain Slan was taking him now.

"We are computing the knowledge of the universe, Dr. Zarkov," Captain Slan said complacently. "We are experimenting with the probabilities of the ideal society. We have already computed over twelve million Utopias. But each of them has been found to have one fatal flaw. So we do not even need to try and build them. The computer tells us what is wrong."

Zarkov stared. "You are absolutely mad, Slan."

"Nonsense! Democracy. Socialism. Marxism. Social democracy. Religious fanaticism. All the world's religions. All the world's philosophies. We have put them to the test in the computer, and each has failed. Now we are working on a combination of the best—to try to find one which has no flaws. And then Ming will rule that society and man's impossible dream will be realized!"

Zarkov was staggered. "You'd let Ming rule a utopia? It would be similar to Satan's rule of heaven."

"With the proper social mechanism, we can create the everlasting society. But we must destroy Arboria, so that Ming will not have to plot and scheme to keep the forest kingdom from blocking his plans. And Ming will be god over the greatest society in the history of the universe." Captain Slan waved a hand. "We started out with these computers years ago. We built most of them here in Mingo, but the machinery proved to be only as effective as the human beings who fed the information into the computers. You see?"

Zarkov frowned. "What are you saying?"

Captain Slan nodded, his eyes gleaming. "I thought that would interest you. And what is the greatest computer in the universe, Dr. Zarkov? Of course, the human brain itself. But as man uses his brain, he is only fulfilling its potential to a mild five or six percent of capacity—if that.

132

Why, many humanoids only think with one or two percent of their brains, maximum!"

They had come to the end of the long aisle. Captain Slan gestured with his head, indicating for Zarkov to follow him around in back of one row of computers.

Zarkov followed.

"My god!" he boomed, turning to stare at Slan. "You're a maniac."

Slan smiled, bowing slightly. "You flatter me, Dr. Zarkov."

Behind each computer, there was a filthy bunk upon which a human being sat staring into space. And attached to the man's skull were dozens of wires, which led into the backs of the computers.

"You've wired these men—"

Slan smiled. "I knew it would be unnecessary to describe it all to you, Dr. Zarkov. You are very perceptive. Yes. Instead of mechanical brains, we use real brains. And these brains in turn operate the computers. These men are the terminals, not the small memory banks of the computers. Yes, Dr. Zarkov. The very best machines in the universe. Human brains."

Zarkov wiped the perspiration from his face.

"We've got very good people here, you know. Most of them with university educations. Scientific geniuses. Doctors." Slan paused and smiled.

"But they're not able to function as human beings," Zarkov commented in horror.

"Of course not, Dr. Zarkov. They must simply be fed and clothed and nurtured like cattle so the machines can use their brains. We treat them decently enough. They have no wills. Total frontal lobotomy has been performed on each of them as the first step in their incorporation into the computer bank, naturally. Their brain cells are free then to perform the instructions fed into the computers to which each is attached. No emotional problems can interfere with their efficient functioning."

"You're totally inhuman," Zarkov gasped, almost unable to speak.

"We must be, to find the world's best social structure, do you not agree, Doctor?"

Zarkov watched the vegetable on the nearest bunk with pity. "Who was he?"

133

"A Professor Burke, as I recall. Captured on board a rocket from Earth years ago. They live longer, you know, without the stress of emotional problems." Slan smiled.

Zarkov almost choked.

"I surmise that you will have a hundred years or more ahead of you, Dr. Zarkov. We consider you our best catch yet, you know." Slan smiled broadly.

"Me?" Zarkov exclaimed, grabbing for his throat. He felt the room spinning around him. "You're going to plug me into one of those computers?"

"Our very best model, Dr. Zarkov," Slan said as his yellow eyes gleamed.

CHAPTER 25

The violet haze lifted and Flash saw a darkened room with rock walls and a stone floor. The faces of the people in the room suddenly became clear enough to see. He strained at the astro-seat, and felt the speed of the pendulum slow down. There was no vibration at all. He stood up.

Three people. Dr. Zarkov. Dale Arden. And a strange girl dressed in hunter's green whom he had never seen before.

"Flash!" Zarkov cried.

"Hi, Doc," Flash said with a grin. "You don't know where I haven't been looking for you."

"Heard you found yourself a time machine, Flash," Zarkov boomed, slapping him on the shoulder. "Come on, let us in on the secret."

Flash turned to Dale. "First, I want to know how you got here, Dale. And when is this? Past or future?"

"Depends," Zarkov said, laughing. "Depends on what point is present." He boomed out in laughter.

"When Kial sent you into time and space, I escaped, Flash," Dale said quickly. "But when I tried to rescue Doc and Sari, the blue men caught me."

134

"Blue men?" Flash frowned.

Zarkov filled him in quickly, identifying Sari.

"And they're going to hook you up to a computer?" Flash cried.

"Right," Zarkov said gloomily. "But it's the very best one." He tried to cheer himself up.

"Doc, you'll blow out the fuse."

"Come on, Flash. That's not nice."

"These blue men—they're going to attack the forest kingdom?"

"Right," Dale said. "Captain Slan has been bragging about that ever since we've been with him."

"It's strange. I happen to know that Ming XIII has sent a team of assassins from three hundred years in the future to kill Prince Barin. That's so Ming and his descendants will rule all the planet."

Dale shrugged. "I'm only telling you what we've been hearing."

"We've got to get you all out of here," Flash said, frowning. "Let me think."

"What about those time belts you've been talking about," Zarkov said. "Just give us one of them."

"Can't," Flash said. "Lari and Kial still have them on."

"I suppose you can mount an assault team and demolish Cerulea. If you can find it, but then it would be too late. I'd be hooked up to the computer by then."

Flash felt the sudden tugging at his flesh. He knew the pendulum was about to swing once again.

"Hurry up," he snapped. "Think of something, Zarkov. The time pendulum is about to move."

"Me!" Zarkov groaned. "I can't think of anything. I've already tried everything. Nothing works."

"Did you pick up that blaster pistol when you fought Kial and Lari on the superway?" Dale asked.

Flash began moving through the air toward the place he had left the astro-seat. "Yes!" He pulled it out of his belt. "Here it is. I hope you can find someway to use it to get out."

"At least it isn't stuck on STUN," Zarkov said contritely.

Flash was in the astro-seat now, and the weight in his lap was very heavy. The metal vibrated. The air shivered about him. There were purple lights.

"Flash—" Dale said. There were tears in her eyes.

"I'll see you safe and sound," Flash said stoutly.

Then the haze came up and he was in it.

He was at rest. The mist was only an illusion. He found himself seated in the astro-chair in the center of the dome of the Tempendulum. He was back to the present.

Outside he could hear laughter

"Well, it's all over, Lari!" Kial cried out. "We've gotten rid of both of them! Dale Arden is in the forest somewhere. And Flash Gordon is caught out there in eternity."

"Good work, Kial. Let's go home."

Kial climbed in through the port and started to jump down to the floor of the dome. His eyes came up and he saw Flash.

He froze.

Lari pushed him forward and Kial fell to the floor. "What's the matter with you, anyway? I almost fell," Lari said.

Then he, too, looked up into Flash's face.

Flash stood above them, hands on hips, a faint smile on his lips.

"Well, well, well," he said contemptuously. "Fancy meeting you two here."

"Uh," said Kial. "It's Gordon."

"It's Flash Gordon, yes. Colonel Gordon, to you, Kial."

"But how did you come back from eternity?" Lari wondered, sitting up and staring at Flash questioningly.

"You forget that if time is reversible, it is also doubly reversible. That is, it can go forward again, too. I simply went forward, and back, and then forward again."

"The Tempendulum," Kial said, "swings both ways, of course."

"He hasn't got his blaster pistol," Lari said quickly. "Use yours, Kial!"

Flash reached out and gripped a handful of Kial's tunic, hauling him up to his feet. "I think that's mine, isn't it?" he said, taking the blaster pistol out of Kial's belt.

"Yes," Kial said nervously. "Yes, it is."

"Now I think you'd better take off that belt, too," said Flash with a smile. "I wouldn't want you coming back here uninvited."

"Oh, yeah," Kial said. He removed the time belt from his waist.

"You, too, Lari," Flash ordered.

"I couldn't do that."

Flash turned the blaster pistol in his direction. "Lari?"

Lari unfastened the belt. He handed it over. Flash took the two belts and studied them.

"I see. Very neat. One pouch for time-travel. One pouch for space-travel. Put them both together and travel through time and space."

"Uh-huh," Kial said.

"But only through the power of this. Right?" Flash pointed to the pendulum and the hovering globe.

"Yeah," Kial admitted unhappily. "What are you going to do to us?"

"Get in the astro-seats," Flash said. "And I'll tell you."

Kial blanched. "No, not to eternity!"

"I said nothing about eternity," Flash said softly. "I'm a firm believer in the old adage that there's no place like home."

"Not back to Ming XIII! I want to stay here," Lari screamed.

"But I don't want you two here," Flash said. "Now move!"

Kial turned and ran out of the dome. He had reached the entry port when Flash caught him by the legs. Kial turned and struck out at Flash. Flash had laid the time belts and his blaster pistol aside. He swung at Kial and hit him solidly on the jaw, knocking him out.

When he turned, Lari held the blaster pistol on him. Lari moved backward out through the port. "Don't touch me, Gordon. I'm going!"

Flash watched. As Lari turned to look where he was stepping through the port, Flash dove for Lari's feet. He grabbed him by the ankles, tripped him, and sent him flying head-first out through the port onto the ground. The blaster pistol sailed through the air and clanged against the side of the big hemisphere.

In a moment, he had Lari neatly laid out beside Kial.

"Now to put these two lunkheads in their astro-seats," Flash muttered as he carried first Lari and then Kial across into the seats under the pendulum.

Soon he had them trussed up in the astro-seats. Then he

137

lifted the heavy heart-shaped weight and screwed it onto the end of the pendulum. Above him, he heard the globe humming and purring.

Flash walked over to the instrument console and stared at the dials and readouts.

He flicked a few switches. When he turned he saw that Kial had just returned to consciousness and was watching him with terrified eyes.

"No!" he shouted. "Not back to Ming! Please—in the name of the seven suns of Mongo!"

"Good-bye, Kial," Flash said sweetly.

Lari woke up and began weeping. "Please, Colonel Gordon. Please let us stay in the forest kingdom. We don't want to go back to Ming XIII."

"Good-bye," Flash said adamantly and threw the switch.

He watched the two astro-seats as he did so.

There was a purple haze, almost instantaneously, and then the two seats and the men in them were gone.

The globe whirred and muttered and moved about in the air lazily. The pendulum trembled.

Flash strapped on one of the time-travel belts and set the readouts to the grid coordinates of the palace.

"Here I come, Prince Barin," he said expectantly, and pressed the space button.

CHAPTER 26

As Flash vanished from sight, Zarkov rubbed his eyes and tugged his beard angrily.

"I never saw anything like it. Wish I'd invented that time gadget."

"Can't we get out of here now, Doc? There's no use staying around any longer, is there?" Dale asked worriedly.

"I suppose not." Zarkov hefted the blaster pistol

thoughtfully. "What do we do with this? Blast our way out, no doubt. But how?"

"Whatever we do, we'd better do it quickly," Sari said impatiently. "I've simply got to get in touch with the intelligence minister."

"Dale, will you and Sari cover the cell door there? I want to try this blaster on the wall. Didn't Flash use this to disintegrate material?"

"Yes," Dale said. "I don't know if it'll work on stones, though. It has to be living matter."

"Oh," Zarkov said disappointedly. "Well, anyway, here goes."

Dale and Sari moved to the cell door and looked out into the corridor. "Go ahead, Doc. There's nobody in sight."

Zarkov flipped on the blaster pistol and aimed it at the stone wall. For a long moment, nothing happened. Then, as he was about to turn it off, he saw a tiny cloud of smoke curling up from the mortar in between the klang rocks.

"That mortar!" Zarkov exclaimed. "Look!"

Dale moved over to the wall. "That's right! There must be something living mixed in with the mortar. Perhaps it's a kind of reconstitutued wood used for adhesive. I don't know how this place is put together, but that mortar seems to be going all right."

Zarkov moved closer to the wall. "Great! I'll burn out all the mortar I can, and then we can loosen the stones and pull them out."

A smell of burning wood and plastic adhesive permeated the air. Sari and Dale kept their eyes glued to the corridor for the appearance of any guards.

"The stench is enough to flush out every man in the colony," Dale said anxiously.

Zarkov laid down the blaster pistol and wrestled with a stone at the lower end of the wall. It gave way and tumbled out onto the floor of the cell.

Beyond the stone lay a wall of mortar.

Zarkov aimed the blaster pistol at the mortar and squeezed hard.

Smoke rose, followed by a foul stench. Suddenly, a bit of light came in from beyond.

"Light!" Zarkov cried. "Look!"

He peered through the hole. He saw gleaming piles of metallic materials, and beyond that something resembling a large airborne saucer.

"Dale," he whispered, moving back into the cell. "We're right next to the flight shop. They've got a space saucer in there."

Dale's eyes widened. "Let's go through."

Zarkov loosened two more stones. There was now crawl-space.

After squirming through, Zarkov pulled Dale and Sari after him. They found themselves in a large deserted workroom filled with flying equipment.

At the end of the assembly line stood a roomy fourcap saucer, that is, a flying saucer with capacity for four passengers. Beyond the work area, a sliding door, made of glass and metal, folded up into the ceiling. It was now closed.

Zarkov moved quickly over to the door and peered out.

"A guard," he hissed, pointing.

Dale looked.

A blue man dressed in the familiar crimson cloak and red skullcap stood at the end of a large flat terrace attached to the flight shop.

Zarkov pondered. "I can zap the guard with the blaster. He'll call someone else, if he has time. By then, we should be able to get this saucer going."

Dale shivered. "Do you really think so?"

"We'll have to find out, won't we?" Zarkov said cheerfully.

He climbed in the saucer and looked at the console. "It's one of those Emperor Ming jobs of five years ago. No problem. It burns lox. And the supply canister is full. Come on, girls, climb in. I'll shove that door open and we'll get out of here before you can say Jack Robinson."

When Zarkov pressed the energizer for the door, it moved silently up into its slot in the ceiling. The movement attracted the guard, who wheeled and walked toward the open flight shop.

Zarkov aimed the blaster in his direction and squeezed the activator. The blue man staggered, threw up his arms, and fell to the ground.

Zarkov ran across the floor to the saucer, jumped through the hatch, and pushed the buttons on the console.

The saucer responded, throbbed, and moved toward the doorway on the lox piles that blasted out from the rocket ports below.

When they emerged onto the terrace outside the flight shop, Zarkov saw that there was unlimited flying space all around. He activated the ascension rockets, the lox piles responded immediately, and the saucer rose into the air.

"Would you look at that!" Zarkov exclaimed, pointing out through the bubbleglass viewport. "They've built their whole plant in a huge pocket of the great jungle."

It was true. The colony of Cerulea was small, but it was spread out in a flat valley that ended abruptly in towering bluffs that rose for hundreds and hundreds of feet. In short, Cerulea was built at the bottom of an enormous pit, perhaps a quarter of a mile below the surface of the earth.

Dale nodded. "It's below the level of the trees, isn't it?"

Zarkov glanced up and saw the sky. "Yes, you see the trees at the top of the pit against the skyline. It's hazy there, too, but you can feel the warmth of the sun. They probably extract some energy from the sun, too."

The saucer moved upward and was now just below the level of the forest around it. They moved into a thicker haze now. It seemed almost greenish in color.

At the landing terrace below them, Zarkov heard a saucer revving up. "They're coming after us," he bellowed. "We've got to hurry."

Suddenly, they were in the air above the forest and there was no more mist. Zarkov glanced down to get his bearings. The city of Cerulea had vanished from sight in a cluster of trees!

Dale gasped. "Doc! The city's gone!"

Zarkov looked down and then he saw that the forest directly below them did not look genuine when examined closely.

"Haze," Zarkov said. "They've camouflaged the whole establishment of Cerulea with a kind of eternal mist."

"And how does that work?" Sari asked.

"From the top, you can't see down into the area where Cerulea lies. I think they've set up projectors on both sides of the area."

"Projectors?" Dale repeated.

"Right. And they're projecting a holograph of a dense woods onto the mist. The three-dimensional picture makes you see trees where they don't exist."

"And that keeps anyone up here from seeing the city down there—but how come we couldn't see the picture above when we were below?" Sari asked.

"The bright sunlight above cuts through the holograph," Zarkov explained. "But from above, looking down into a darkened pit, the holograph is backed up by a black background and all you see is the woods of the projected visualization."

"But why go to all that trouble?" Dale asked in confusion.

"Secrecy," Sari responded. "We've been looking for them for a long time. I mean, the prince's agents."

"Right," Zarkov agreed. He peered down into the forest and saw a wavering silver line. "There's the superway. We haven't far to go."

"Are you heading for Arboria?" Sari asked.

"No, I want to see that Tempendulum. Scientific curiosity." Zarkov grinned.

"You're not the only one," Sari said.

"Huh?"

She pointed to the rear of the saucer. Zarkov peered out. He saw two shapes—gleaming golden shapes in the form of flat poker chips. Two more flying vehicles.

"They're following us," Dale said nervously.

Zarkov nodded curtly.

CHAPTER 27

Prince Barin slowly crumpled the paper in his hand and held it in front of his chest. He turned to Minister Hamf and spoke sharply.

"Blue men, indeed. Who sent out this madman's message?"

Hamf was properly deferential. "It was one of my most trusted agents, Your Excellency."

"Indeed," Barin snapped. "Zarkov warned me to pay attention to your reports. Perhaps I should." He thrust his hands behind him and paced back and forth a moment. "And where is Zarkov, anyway? He went out of here hours ago, said he'd keep in touch, and I haven't heard a word from him."

"I've been keeping the lines of communication open, sire," Hamf said.

"Any word of Flash Gordon and Dale Arden?" Prince Barin asked hopefully. He crossed to the window to look down into the capital's square.

"No, Your Excellency," Hamf said regretfully. "Perhaps they, too, fell into the hands of this strange group of undesirables."

"Perhaps, perhaps," Prince Barin said impatiently. "I don't know what to think about this. What am I to do—postpone the ceremonies which start in twenty minutes? Send out a scouting expedition to wipe out these blue men your man has found? Tell me, Hamf, what do I do?"

Hamf shook his head. "It's a difficult decision to make, Your Excellency. Although we have known for some time that there was a buildup of undesirables in the forest kingdom, we have been unable to spot where they might live. Now that we know there are those blue men—wherever they come from—we do not yet know where they now live."

"Fine, fine," Barin replied sarcastically. "Then we've nothing to go on. I simply cannot cancel the celebration. It would raise too many eyebrows in the kingdom. They'd think something serious is happening to the government."

Hamf murmured contritely, "Yes, Your Excellency."

"Oh, go on—get out of here! And don't come back until you can bring me some good news about Zarkov or Flash Gordon. Or *something* decent."

Hamf bowed and removed himself quickly from the throne room. Prince Barin stood at the window and gazed out over the crowd in the square. The people seemed to be massing in large numbers. It was obvious that they wanted to celebrate the liberation of the entire planet of Mongo from the grip of Ming the Merciless.

Prince Barin glanced at his digital clock by the window

and noted that he had only a few more minutes before he was scheduled to make his appearance.

He turned and at that instant the door opened once again. Hamf was back.

"Didn't I tell you not to come back here until you could bring me good news?" Prince Barin demanded.

Hamf said nothing, but simply stepped to one side.

Flash Gordon strode in, his blond hair glistening in the light.

"Prince Barin," Flash cried, extending his right hand and striding vigorously across the palace floor.

"Flash!" Prince Barin cried, his voice friendly and his good nature restored. "You're here at last!"

"Had a few minor delays on the way," Flash replied, grinning.

"And where is the beautiful Dale Arden?" Prince Barin asked in his courtly way.

"It's a complicated story," Flash said, stroking his chin. "But she's safe. I do know that."

Prince Barin laughed. "Dr. Zarkov was so worried about you that he went out in an airscout to find you."

"I know," Flash said quietly.

"You've seen him?" Prince Barin asked in surprise.

"Yes," said Flash. "He's with Dale. And a girl named Sari."

Hamf cleared his throat at the doorway. "She's one of mine."

Prince Barin turned in annoyance. "Are you still here? I thought I told you to go back to your decoder machines."

"Yes, sire," Hamf said obsequiously, and bowed himself out again.

"Well," asked Prince Barin, "where are Dale and Zarkov?"

Flash cleared his throat. "Prince Barin, sit down for a moment, will you? This isn't a simple story that I'm going to tell you."

Prince Barin frowned. "If I must, I must."

"You must—if you want to hear the truth," Flash said gently.

They sat together in cellulogorm chairs at the side of the room and Flash told Prince Barin as tersely and as completely as he could what had happened not only to him but to Dale and to Dr. Zarkov and to Sari as well.

Prince Barin was visibly aroused when Flash had finished. He rose and paced back and forth in agitation.

"Good lord! It simply doesn't seem possible! Men from the future? Blue warriors from Ming's laboratories? All trying to destroy the forest kingdom."

"It's possible, all right," Flash said gravely. "Now we've got to act."

Prince Barin nodded. "I'm going out there and announce to my people that we have been having a great deal of trouble on the border. I'm sure they'll support me if I call for troops and military supplies."

Flash held up his hand. "No, I don't want you to go out there at all."

Prince Barin's chest swelled out. "I'm the ruler of this kingdom, Flash. I *must* go out there."

"I don't mean to contradict you, Prince Barin," Flash said slowly. "You've got to remember I'm from a democracy where we all have our say. I want you to let me go out there on that balcony. Then we'll see what Ming XIII's henchmen do."

Prince Barin's eyes lighted up. "I see what you mean! When they see Flash Gordon, the man Ming XIII had promised to take care of, they might—"

"—might kill me," Flash interrupted, smiling.

Prince Barin frowned. "Let's see how they react," he said. He stepped over to the window and looked down on the square. Thousands of forest-kingdom people milled about, looking up toward the balcony where Prince Barin soon would appear.

Flash stood beside Prince Barin. He turned to shake hands with him.

"Good luck, Flash," Prince Barin said.

Flash stepped through the French windows and walked across the balcony to the railing.

He raised a hand in salute to the people.

Wild cheering broke out in the large crowd. They knew Flash Gordon. "Flash!" they cried. "Flash!"

Flash smiled and raised his hand again. His eyes moved over the crowd, trying to spot anyone who might resemble in dress or aspect either Kial or Lari. He did not see anyone.

He took a deep breath and spoke.

A hushed silence fell over the crowd.

Now, thought Flash. If they're going to kill me, now is the time. . . .

CHAPTER 28

Orto was a young man in his twenties. Lanl was an older man, at least fifty. Both wore a disguise of hunter's green. Both felt uncomfortable. Both stood in the crowd of forest-kingdom people who waited for the scheduled appearance of Prince Barin on the palace balcony.

Orto glanced around nervously. "I don't like it, Lanl. There's something not quite right."

"You're young. You're eager. You're unnerved. Don't be that way. This is a waiting game. If you're not up to it, let me do the job."

Orto shook his head vigorously. "I'm still worried about Gordon."

"Gordon, Gordon," Lanl said disgustedly. "What's so big about Gordon?"

"He's written up in all our history books as the greatest liberator ever to hit Mongo."

"Books are written by knaves and fools," Lanl said cheerfully. "We'll take care of history. Just follow orders and we'll get Prince Barin. In spite of the readouts in the Annals of Time."

"Aren't you afraid of Gordon?"

"Certainly, I'm afraid of Gordon. Didn't I insist that Ming have him taken care of by another time probe?"

"Well, then. Do you believe Ming succeeded?"

Lanl shrugged. "We have to believe in something, don't we, Orto?"

Orto glanced furtively around. "Shh! I think people are listening to us."

"Then let's not talk," Lanl ordered.

He stared up at the balcony where Prince Barin would

appear. A flash of light reflected on a glass pane as someone opened the French doors.

"Here he comes!" a spectator shouted.

Lanl jabbed Orto in the ribs. "Come on."

Orto nodded. He moved quickly with the older man to the edge of the crowd. Lanl had removed a small miniray pistol from his tunic. Orto had one, too. They stood by a wall and waited.

No one noticed them.

No one saw the miniray pistols, for they were no larger than a ballpoint pen.

The balcony doors opened and a figure stepped into the sunlight. Bright-yellow hair caught the light.

"Yellow hair," Lanl said in a choked voice.

"It's not Barin!"

"It's Gordon," Lanl whispered. He shoved the miniray pistol into his tunic and grabbed Orto's arm. "You were right. The probe team didn't take care of Grdoon."

"Then the tape readout is true. Gordon survived whatever tactics Ming XIII brought to bear."

Lanl nodded, his eyes narrowed. "Let's get out of here."

"Where to?"

"The Tempendulum. I want to get back to Ming to explain what happened."

"You think he'll believe it?"

Lanl shook his head. "We'll have to talk fast."

"Flash! Flash!" the crowd chanted in unison.

"My friends," Flash Gordon said over the loudspeaker. "On an occasion like today, words are inadequate to express my affection and love for the people of the forest kingdom."

Orto and Lanl moved quickly away from the crowd and ran through a side street.

"Guards!" a voice shouted suddenly, booming out over the sound of the crowd responding to Flash's speech. "Seize those men!"

It was Flash Gordon's voice on the loudspeaker, interrupting his own speech.

Orto turned to Lanl. "He's spotted us."

They raced down the alley and turned at the corner. The safety of the woods lay not fifty feet away.

But a big guard blocked their way; he was dressed in

147

forest green and wore a peaked cap. He had his enormous hands on his wide hips.

"Be ye in a terrible hurry, fellows?" the big man asked with a broad smile.

Orto stumbled over the big man's feet in his haste to flee. Lanl tried to get away from the big man's hands, but ended up in their grasp.

Another large guard then joined the first.

"What have ye here, anyway? A pair of runaways?"

"Aye," answered the first.

"The prophesy was right," Orto said, sighing.

Lanl shook his head. "Well, maybe it's all for the best. I wouldn't want to face Ming XIII without proof Prince Barin was dead."

The big guard prodded them both in the back. "Move it fast. Ye're going to see the prince, but first let's search ye to see if ye're carrying weapons."

Orto looked at Lanl with an expression of hopelessness. A moment later, they had no weapons at all. The big guard had the miniray pistols in his pocket.

CHAPTER 29

Dale peered through the bubbleglass viewport of the fourcap saucer and pointed in triumph.

"There it is, Doc. You see that gleam of metal in the trees?"

Zarkov leaned forward, peering intently. "Righto, Dale. Good girl. Okay, let's make a descent and get this saucer on the ground. This is an old crate and I don't want to have trouble with it the way I had with my airscout."

Zarkov grinned and fiddled with the controls on the small console.

The saucer dropped toward the treetops.

"Sari, would you look out the aft port and see if those clowns have picked up our trail again?"

Sari moved in her seat and squinted out through the

rear viewport. Zarkov had gone through some exhaustive tactical maneuvers to evade their pursuers. Apparently, he had shaken them off. In doing so, he had almost taken off the saucer's radar antenna on one of the high conifers.

"No sign of them, Dr. Zarkov."

"Good, good," Zarkov muttered, pleased, peering through the bubbleglass at the forest as it rapidly rose toward them.

"There's a clearing around the Tempendulum," Dale said.

"I see it, Dale. Thanks."

Zarkov thrust the guidance disc forward and the saucer moved downward, slanting from fore to aft in a direct line to the estimated point of arrival. In seconds, the saucer had settled carefully on the retrothrust pile.

Zarkov flipped off the switches, slipped the dogs on the hatch, and jumped to the ground. He reached up and helped Dale and Sari down.

"Sari, you keep one eye peeled in that eastern sky, will you? I don't want those blue men to come up here and surprise me. I want to give my full attention to this alleged time machine."

"Right, Dr. Zarkov," Sari said. She climbed the metal ladder to the top of the minisaucer and perched on its apex. Her eyes shaded by one hand, she sat and waited.

"Come on, Dale," Zarkov said eagerly. "Show me the inside of this dome."

Dale nodded and they hurried across the clearing to the open port. Dale pointed and Zarkov went in first, helping Dale in after him.

With mounting excitement and astonishment, Zarkov gazed about him. His eyes lit first on the pendulum hanging from the ceiling of the dome, the heart-shaped weight now once again attached to the bottom. Then he took in the floating globe of opaque black that hummed softly near the pendulum.

In moments, he was at the console, gazing in fascination at the gauges, dials, and readout ports.

"How about that?" he muttered to himself.

Dale came closer, looking over his shoulder. "Flash and I tried to figure out what they all meant."

"Well, I don't know myself," Zarkov said abstractedly, stroking his beard. "But if we're correct, and it is a time-travel operation, it's obvious that the controls have to do with time, the speed of light, and velocity. Right?"

"Right, Doc," Dale said uncertainly.

"So," Zarkov said, "here's the time control. That's fairly obvious."

"T.C.," mused Dale. "We guessed that right."

"And velocity regulator, that seems obvious, too, doesn't it?"

"To you, Doc." Dale sighed. "We didn't get that."

"Velocity means speed multiplied by the weight of the object, of course, to quote a bit of elementary physics." Zarkov grinned. "You would have to regulate the speed with the weight of the object transmitted. Too much speed would crush a large object; too little speed would cause a smaller object to explode."

"Oh," Dale said, impressed.

"And E.T.Z. is also obvious."

"It is?" Dale asked, bewildered.

"Sure. Estimated time zone. Say you've got to predict the particular area of time in which you're going to travel. Well, you've got to have good controls to get you near the right century. The rest of the controls are actually refinements to that one. Once you're in your zone, then you clutch into your time-control mechanism, which seems to be the second gear, say, year five of the hundred-year zone from the E.T.Z. Then you got to predict the particular area of time in which you're going to travel. Well, you've got to have good controls to get you near the right century. The rest of the controls are actually refinements of that one. Once you're in your zone, then you clutch into your time-control mechanism, which seems to be the second gear, say, year five of the hundred-year zone from the E.T.Z. Then you go to your velocity regulator once you've gotten to the proper year. It's a simple clutch mechanism, dealing with time rather than with space."

"I see," Dale said slowly.

"Marvelous," Zarkov muttered, checking through the readout ports and studying the gauges with their golden needles.

"Doc," Dale said tentatively.

"What is it, Dale?" Zarkov asked distractedly.

"Can I ask you a question?"

"Shoot."

"What's that opaque black globe?"

Zarkov rose reluctantly from the console and moved to the center of the dome. He looked up at the globe which floated near his head.

"Dale," he boomed out, "that's the heart of the whole operation."

"Oh?" Dale was impressed. "I thought the pendulum was."

"The pendulum is the secondary part," Zarkov explained condescendingly. "But this is the conversion unit."

"What does it convert?"

"I'd guess those scientists had figured a way to trap time. I mean you've got to gain control over time to travel through it, haven't you?"

"Yes, but—"

"Look at it this way, Dale. Einstein trapped energy when he equated energy to mass times the speed of light. Right?"

"If you say so," Dale replied.

"That freed the energy in the atom. All right. Since that time, scientists have been trying to free time from the strictures of our three-dimensional space. You take Einstein's equation, $e = mc^2$, and you can see that the next thing to be freed from that equation is time itself."

"I don't see that because I don't see time mentioned at all in the formula."

"It's locked in the c^2 factor—the constant speed of light."

"What has that to do with time?"

"The symbol c means the speed of light. That's 186,000 miles per second. If you break up the speed of light into its elements, you get $c = d/t$. That is, the speed of light equals the distance traveled divided by the time involved. Right?"

"I suppose so," Dale said.

"Somehow these scientists have managed to speed up light so that its velocity isn't constant—so that it exceeds c. That is, if you speed light up to say 392,000 miles per second, light would arrive at a specific destination in half the time. Meaning that you've actually divided time in two. Right?"

151

"Yes," Dale said, now thoroughly perplexed. "I think so."

"And so, if you can speed up light, you can also slow down time. And if you can slow down light, you can speed up time. And so you can control time by speeding up light, or through manipulation of energy and mass, the other part of the Einstein equation. That is, you break down what is a constant into its component parts, and control each part. Then you can control time and use it to your own purposes. And if you can control the speed of time, you must be able to control its direction as well. Q.E.D."

"But how?"

"That's for them to say, Dale. But they've done it, and in that floating globe lies the answer. Scientists broke the secret of the atom with nuclear fission. These chaps have come up with something to speed up light and thus free time from its strictures. The secret is in there." Zarkov's eyes gleamed. "And it's obviously working."

"Dr. Zarkov," Sari's called from outside. "Come here. There's a strange craft circling above us."

Zarkov ran out into the clearing. He squinted up into the sky.

"Relax," he cried gleefully. "It's one of Prince Barin's aircruisers. We're among friends."

Five minutes later, Flash, Prince Barin, Intelligence Minister Hamf and Orto and Lanl stood inside the dome of the Tempendulum as Zarkov paced up and down, lecturing to Flash and Prince Barin and occasionally turning to interrogate the two prisoners.

"You mean to say you know nothing about the workings of this time machine?" Zarkov boomed angrily. "What kind of agents are you, anyway? Don't you know anything?"

"We're not totally ignorant," Lanl said, his eyes narrowing and his temper flaring. "It's not our specialty, this kind of scientific gibberish. We were sent here to do a job."

Orto stared morosely at the floor. "And we failed."

"I don't even know what you're talking about," Lanl said to Zarkov. "We don't know how it works, but we do know it does. It's a completely radical departure from our early time machines. You're the scientist. Why don't you figure it out?"

Zarkov wheeled away and paced back and forth, fuming and muttering to himself.

Flash faced Lanl. "But you do admit you were sent here to assassinate Prince Barin?"

Lanl turned to look at Prince Barin, who gazed at him unflinchingly. "Yes."

"Why?"

"Obviously so that the forest kingdom could not be consolidated. In our time—Ming XIII's time—we have continuous trouble with President Barin's country."

"President Barin," Prince Barin muttered with a faint smile.

"Your descendant, obviously," Flash said goodnaturedly. "Note that the present monarchy will be changed to a constitutional democracy with the substitution of the word president for prince."

Prince Barin waved a hand easily.

"By returning in time," Lanl continued stiffly, "Ming XIII attempted to kill Prince Barin, thus weakening the social structure of the forest kingdom, and allow Ming the Merciless to bring it to heel. Except for Flash Gordon—"

"Kial and Lari were sent to stop me from getting to Arboria," Flash told Prince Barin. "You see how obvious it all is?"

Zarkov wheeled and came toward Lanl. "What about the blue men? How do they fit in?"

Lanl's eyes narrowed. "In our computer research, we discovered a hidden army in the forests of Arboria. They were called blue men in the Annals of Time. We didn't know why, really. They may be the hidden contingent that Ming the Merciless counted on to take Arboria."

Zarkov stroked his beard. "I see. But what happened to them?"

"We never could discover that in the historical readouts," Lanl admitted. "That's why Ming XIII sent a third time probe to work with them."

"You mean we've got to isolate another pair of your murderous hoodlums from the future?" Zarkov boomed indignantly.

Lanl smiled faintly. "I'm afraid that's right, Kazov."

"Damn it, it's Zarkov!" Zarkov snapped. "What's wrong

with you nitwits? Can't anybody pronounce my name right?"

Flash moved in between Zarkov and Lanl. "Cool it, you two," he ordered. "Get in those astro-seats. You're going back to Ming XIII and report your failure."

Lanl's face tightened. "Perhaps we could deal."

Flash laughed harshly. "No deal, Lanl. How could we trust you?"

"Wait," Prince Barin said. "Zarkov, could you use these men? I mean could they be questioned for scientific information?"

Orto nodded eagerly. "We'd be glad to tell you what we know, Dr. Vokoff."

"The damned fools don't even know how this machine works," Zarkov said disgustedly. "What good would they do me? No dice, Prince Barin."

Barin frowned. "I like to be fair."

"Fair?" Zarkov cried. "These two killers were sent here to murder you in cold blood and you want to set them up in your palace as emissaries from the future? Bah!"

Flash looked steadily at Prince Barin. "Perhaps Doc is right, Prince Barin."

"We'd be glad to cooperate," Lanl said tensely. There was perspiration on his forehead.

Flash made up his mind. "Get in the seats, gentlemen. We haven't all day."

Reluctantly Lanl and Orto climbed into the seats and Flash fastened the straps. Zarkov hurried over to the console and manipulated the digital readouts.

"Perhaps just one more chance," Lanl said in a low voice. "Could we bargain for a life here in your prison compound?"

Prince Barin shook his head sadly. "I'm afraid not, sorry."

"Zarkov," Flash said quickly.

Zarkov turned, noted Lanl and Orto in their astro-seats, and pulled the big switch.

A buzzing and humming followed, the floating globe seemed to flash and vibrate internally, the pendulum glowed and trembled, and a purple haze enveloped the two seats.

When it cleared moments later, the two would-be assassins were gone.

154

"I'll be damned," Zarkov marveled.

"Good-bye Orto, good-bye Lanl," Prince Barin said sadly.

"You've too much sympathy for knaves," Zarkov snapped.

"Perhaps," Prince Barin said softly.

The entire dome around them trembled suddenly, then shook almost as if a tremendous earthquake had jostled it. The metallic integument rattled as if it were being shaken by some harsh force of nature. There was a high-pitched screeching that assailed the ears of everyone inside the dome.

"The neutralizer ray!" Flash yelled, clapping his hands to his ears.

Now came the strange odor that Flash and Dale had smelled before on the superway in the jetcar just before it had cracked up.

"Somebody's activating that antimatter gun," exclaimed Flash. "We'll be atomized!"

"The blue men!" Dale cried. "They followed us. They found that ray gun and they've turned it on the dome."

Zarkov turned from the console and stared up at the dome above him. "Look, it's simply disintegrating! It's turning into nothing."

"Doc!" Flash yelled, grabbing Dale and running across the floor to the astro-seats. "Ten minutes! Flick the switch to minus ten minutes. You hear me? Minus ten em. One oh em."

Then there was oblivion.

CHAPTER 30

And there they were, Flash and Dale, ten minutes earlier in the Tempendulum with the rest of the crowd in the time dome, too, listening to Flash interrogate Lanl.

It was odd, seeing himself over there ten minutes before.

"Quick," Flash said to Dale. "Let's get out of here."

Dale followed him, skirting the group—the other Dale of ten minutes ago among them—who listened to Flash and Lanl.

No one noticed them as they ran out into the clearing.

"This is the same way I was able to knock out Kial and Lari," Flash said laughing.

"Yes," Dale said. "I understand now."

"Where is that antimatter gun? You said you had seen it, didn't you?"

"Yes. When I was running from Kial and Lari, I happened right by it. It was covered with branches."

"Lead me to it."

"You think the blue men are there?"

"I think they'll be there soon, and when they get there, we're going to stop them from destroying the time dome and us."

They ran through the trees.

"There," Dale said, pointing.

Flash turned and followed her extended arm. They passed through two narrow trees, an outcrop of klang rock, and there was the large laser gun, covered with tree branches.

"Good," Flash said. He pulled Dale aside. "We've got to hide and—"

They heard voices.

"The fools didn't know I monitored their call. I've got every word they said and I know all about that laser gun. Brod, we'll simply aim it at the Tempendulum and destroy them all."

It was Captain Slan's voice.

Flash gestured to Dale. The two of them moved in behind a thick polypody fern twenty feet high and hid there.

Slan and Brod trampled through the underbrush.

"Here it is, Brod. Help me get these branches off. It's a brilliant way to get rid of them all."

Brod chuckled. "It's a good thing we intercepted the messages from that flight Prince Barin and Gordon made to the Tempendulum. That's the only time we could get them all together at once."

Flash put his mouth to Dale's ear. "They know everyone is in the Tempendulum."

"They obviously tracked Zarkov in the saucer."

Flash nodded.

"It's all set," Slan said.

Peering out, Flash saw the blue man peeping through the magniscopic sights.

"Swing it around the other way," he instructed Brod.

Brod complied. The two of them swung the big laser rod around until it pointed at the Tempendulum, which could barely be seen through the forest growth.

"They're aiming it now," Flash whispered.

"What do we do?" Dale asked fearfully.

Flash got out his blaster pistol and moved through the undergrowth. "Stay here."

Dale shook her head. "I'm coming with you."

Flash shrugged.

"Okay," Slan said, his blue face wreathed in a big grin, his wicked yellow teeth showing against the indigo background. "I've got the Tempendulum zeroed in. Get back here, Brod, and we'll get rid of the whole bunch of them. And Ming can take over Arboria."

Brod cackled in glee, rubbing his hands together.

Flash stepped out of the undergrowth.

"Take your hands off that laser rod," he commanded.

Slan turned, his eyes wide with surprise. "Huh? You? Gordon?"

"Me. Gordon." Flash smiled. "Up with the hands, Slan."

"How'd you get out here? We saw you inside that dome," Brod complained.

"Magic." Flash grinned.

"Magic like you used to get Zarkov and the girls out of that cell, eh?" Slan grated out.

"That's right."

Slan reached for the activator button on the laser rod.

Flash squeezed the grip of the blaster pistol. Instantly, Slan was frozen, reaching out for the activator button. Flash turned the blaster pistol and squeezed the hand grip at Brod. Brod froze in his tracks, stunned into immobility.

"Come on, Dale," Flash said. "We've got to get these two back to the dome."

Dale nodded. "Are they unconscious?"

"No. Only frozen. That means they're able to move, but not able to talk, think, or act on their own. It's the first and lightest phase of blaster intensity."

Dale took Brod by the arm as Flash guided Slan along

157

past the ray gun. The blue men neither said anything nor protested in the slightest. Their yellow eyes focused blankly in front of them.

Flash led Slan into the dome and Dale brought Brod with her.

"Hold it, everybody," Flash yelled.

Instantly the dome was silent.

"Who's that?" Prince Barin asked.

"The blue men," Flash said.

"That's Slan," Zarkov snapped.

"And Brod," Sari said.

Flash nodded. He led Slan over to the astro-seat.

"What are you going to do to them?"

"Send them ahead in time." Flash smiled in satisfaction. "Then we won't be bothered with them any more."

Flash strapped in Slan, and Dale pulled the leather tight on Brod.

"Captain Slan," Flash said, "there was something about a third time probe. It was sent down to investigate your operation in Cerulea. Do you know anything about that?"

Slan said nothing. He did not look at Flash.

Zarkov pushed forward, booming out, "You've got him on freeze, Flash. Bring him out of it, or he won't say a word."

Flash nodded, stepped forward, and slapped Slan lightly on the face.

"Captain Slan!" he cried.

Slan's eyes flickered. He stared about him in consternation. Then his eyes moved to the ceiling of the dome.

"We destroyed the dome! How——?"

"Not quite yet," Flash said with a faint smile.

"I don't get it," Brod growled.

"What happened to the two men who came in from Ming XIII to Cerulea?"

Slan laughed. "Those nuts? They claimed they were from three hundred years in the future."

"Then you did find them?"

"They found us." Slan laughed unpleasantly. "They were harmless nuts. We hooked them up to the computers."

Flash glanced at Zarkov. He smiled at Slan. "It might interest you to know that they weren't crazy at all."

"No?" Slan frowned. "I don't believe it."

"Well, we'll prove it to you. Would you like that?" Flash asked softly.

Slan glanced at Brod and then back at Flash. He blustered. "Well, sure, if that's the way you want it, then prove it."

Flash waved to Zarkov. "Over on the switch, Doc. All right, Slan, in less than thirty seconds, you'll have a chance to explain to Ming XIII why you debrained his top probe team and hooked them up to the computers."

"Ming XIII?" Slan exclaimed, his face covered with perspiration. "What are you raving about?"

"Doc!"

The switch moved quickly.

A trembling filled the air inside the dome, the pendulum trembled, and the opaque black globe sizzled.

Violet haze enveloped the two blue men.

"Hey, what is this?" Slan cried out. "What are you doing?"

And then they were gone.

"All right," Flash cried. "Everybody out of this place. We're going to blow it off the face of the planet. We don't want any more minions of Ming XIII visiting us."

They ran out through the port and Flash walked to the laser rod antimatter gun.

Hours later, Prince Barin and Flash and Zarkov were in consultation in the palace.

"I don't really know what to do with Cerulea and those blue men," Prince Barin said sadly.

"I don't think you've got anything to worry about, Prince Barin," said Zarkov. "They're simply one-generation men, not selectively bred to produce offspring, but simply bred to fight. If there's no one to lead them, and if they die out, simply exile them to the Boiling Desert, or the Ultimate Icepack, send them in food, and let them live out their days."

Prince Barin sighed. "Even clowns like them should have more to live for than that."

"Well," Zarkov said sympathetically, "we know where Cerulea is. We can get them out of there and simply fill in the pit. Then we can test one or two of the blue men out, keeping the rest under surveillance, and see if we can turn them into useful citizens of the forest kingdom."

Prince Barin nodded. "I like the sound of that much better, Zarkov."

Flash spoke up. "Why don't you put them to work for Zarkov in the lab? They're well versed in computer techniques."

"Very good." Prince Barin smiled.

Flash turned to Dale, who had been engaged in small talk with Sari.

"I'm hungry, Dale. How about you and Sari?"

"Right. It's been a long day."

"Let's go have dinner and see the latest holograph at the Capital Theater."

"Okay," Dale said happily. "You coming, Doc?"

Zarkov nodded. "Yeah. Sari? Be my guest." He paused as they started out through the door. "Hey, what's playing, anyway?"

Prince Barin had followed them to the door and now smiled. "It's an old H. G. Wells historical. Called *The Time Machine*."

Zarkov groaned. "Oh, no! Not science fiction!"

"Oh, yes," replied Prince Barin, laughing. "Good viewing!"